A DEADLY DECEPTION

MARGARET THOMSON
DAVIS

A DEADLY
DECEPTION

B&W PUBLISHING

First published 2005
This paperback edition
first published 2006
by B&W Publishing Ltd
99 Giles Street, Edinburgh EH6 6BZ

ISBN 13 9 781845 020897

ISBN 10 1 84502 089 8

British Library Cataloguing in Publication Data:
A catalogue record for this book is available from
the British Library

Printed and bound by Nørhaven Paperback A/S

ACKNOWLEDGEMENTS

The following people helped me with the research for this book and, to them, I am very grateful.

The dedicated people of Women's Aid, especially Evelyn Shaw and Carol Mundy.

As usual, police officers were very generous with their help and advice. On this occasion, because of the unexpected way the story worked out, I didn't need to use most of what they told me. Nevertheless, I must express special gratitude to Detective Superintendent Stephen Heath who was a great help with the telephone idea in the plot.

Many thanks also to Detective Inspector Bannerman, Constable Gerry McEwan and Constable Alan Meikle.

I don't know the name of the concierge at the Red Road high-rise flats but I'd like to thank him for his patience in showing me around and answering all my questions.

DEDICATION

I always believed that an angel was a flimsy, ethereal creature. Now I've discovered that she is a very down-to-earth, plain-spoken Glasgow woman with a great sense of humour.

Her name is Evelyn Pullar. Evelyn works as a sheltered housing manager and is much admired and loved by everyone in her care.

I dedicate this book to her with heartfelt thanks.

I

Talk about easy money? This was easy money all right. And nobody knew. That was the beauty of it. Nobody knew. Mabel Smith squeezed herself tightly together and mentally rubbed her hands. Oh, how she'd blessed the day she'd been sitting in the doctor's waiting room and picked up one of the magazines spread over the coffee table. The table had cloudy patches and rings made by cups, and initials scratched on it, no doubt by one of the many young criminals in the area. The magazines were tattered, out of date, the covers gaudy with pictures of flashy cars and motorbikes.

She had been alone in the waiting room and had begun leafing through one of the magazines to pass the time. It was the back pages that caught her eye. Shocked her eye. She'd never seen such pictures before in all of her long life. Not even on television. They weren't just of naked or half-naked girls, but girls posing open-legged and touching themselves. She was hypnotised by the pictures and could not believe the filthy words accompanying them. Here was a world she had never even guessed existed. Never in a million years. Not knowing exactly why, she crushed one of the magazines into her handbag, then sat rigid-backed with burning face and pulse racing, waiting for the receptionist to call her into the surgery.

Later, at home, she studied the back pages and, after having made sure that a photograph was not necessary and real identities could not be traced, she wrote to one of the box numbers, an agency. By return, she was given a private telephone number and it was explained to her exactly how she would be paid.

Talk about easy money? Such a good addition to her pension. All she ever needed to do was talk. And listen, of course. Often she had to listen. At first, she had been terrified. Paralysed with terror. She had to keep silently repeating words in her head. 'No one knows. No one can ever find out. This will always be my very secret life.'

Gradually, she had become successful, not so much in a dirty way. She persuaded herself that she was being more romantic than anything else. There was one man in particular with whom she had managed to become more confident and intimate. He just seemed lonely, poor thing, and in need of comfort and love. Not like some of the others, who sounded so enthusiastically disgusting and then furious if she didn't respond in equally explicit and filthy terms.

The lonely man's name was John, although it might not be his real name – just as Angela, the name she gave him, was not real. It was not a real world they were inhabiting on the phone. She was sure he realised that, just as she did.

He phoned her every evening between 6 and 7 p.m. She pretended she had to go out after that, but in fact she didn't want to miss *Coronation Street*. She had become very involved with the lives of the *Coronation Street* characters.

Eventually she and John became like friends, as well as telephone lovers. He didn't seem to mind the cost. They began calling each other 'darling' or 'my love' or 'my dearest love'.

She really enjoyed the calls. She had plucked up courage to use sexual imagery and even enjoyed that now. He did too. He responded in kind and they both had orgasms as a result.

2

It was as if they were intimate in every way and yet they had never even set eyes on each other.

He began to ask her what she looked like and she certainly couldn't tell him about her pebble-thick lenses and her crippling arthritis. She thought, however, there wouldn't be any harm in enjoying this extension of their romantic fantasy.

'I'm about five foot six,' she said. 'I'm quite curvaceous, with long blonde hair, blue eyes, and quite full, pouty lips.'

'What are you wearing just now?' he asked.

'One of those very short denim miniskirts and a low-cut . . .' she laughed, 'a very low-cut pale blue top with the letters fcuk embroidered on it. The top is a bit tight because I've quite a large bust.'

He became quite excited, as she knew he would. Now he asked, 'Is your hair long?'

'Oh, yes. I sometimes have it held up by combs stuck in at the back, sometimes by frilly covered elastic bands, sometimes tied back with a ribbon. Blue usually. Blue's my favourite colour.'

They had regular conversations like that now. Each time she'd describe a different outfit, short tops that showed part of her belly above low-cut denim trousers and teeteringly high-heeled sandals.

But then he began asking if they could meet. Meet in real life. Oh no. Definitely not, she'd told him.

'The whole point of all this is complete confidentiality. We can relax and be at ease and completely ourselves.' And make some money, she could have said but didn't.

Meeting him would put a stop to that and she needed the money. It was safer this way anyway. She'd learned a thing or two about men since she'd started the phone business. Most of the other men who phoned were really terrible, like beasts, monsters, and certainly not to be trusted. Admittedly John sounded different but you never knew . . . Best to be on the safe side. Anyway, the money was such a consideration.

She tried to talk him out of the idea.

'We're perfectly happy as we are,' she insisted.

He wasn't, apparently. Not any more. He pleaded with her. She remained firm.

'I don't want to risk spoiling our relationship,' she said. 'It's so perfect for me and I really thought it was for you too.'

But it wasn't, apparently.

Every time he phoned her now, at some point in the conversation he brought up the subject of getting together in person. Now she was beginning to almost dread his calls rather than enjoy them. It wasn't that she blamed him. She understood how he felt. Nevertheless he was beginning to spoil what for her had truly been a perfect set-up. She really did enjoy it.

Now every time the phone rang, it made her sigh. It would be ringing again soon, she knew. She went over to the window and gazed out at the scene below. Her flat was in one of the high-rise buildings on the Balgray Hill in the Balornock district of Glasgow. Her building was called The Heights. The flats on the other side of the building enjoyed a magnificent view over the city and far beyond to the distant hills. But her windows – the sitting room and bedroom to the front and the kitchen to the side – had no such pleasant outlook. Well, there was a view over Springburn Park but it was partly blocked at the front by other tower buildings. There was an entrance to the park a bit further down and she sometimes ventured into the park for a walk. There were so many thugs and vandals and gangs roaming about the area, however, that she didn't feel safe. She had a thing about safety. A phobia, you might even call it. Who could blame her in a place like this?

She went through to the kitchen to make herself a cup of coffee and gazed from the window as she filled the kettle at

4

the sink. There had once been a few shops further along. Now there was a notice which warned, 'Dangerous building. Keep out'. The place was falling to bits. Had been for ages. Rubbish swirled around and the walls were covered in graffiti. There were a few shabby-looking shops still further along, also much decorated by graffiti. She hated having to go into them. It was so much better to catch the bus into town and get decent food from Marks & Spencer's. She always bought her food there now. Marks & Spencer's wasn't cheap, however. That was one of the reasons for continuing to talk with John on the phone. She never used to be able to afford Marks & Spencer's food.

As she went through the long lobby from the kitchen to the sitting room, she heard bawling and screaming outside. She flinched nervously. She could never get used to the noise and the outbreaks of violence in the place. Everybody just minded their own business and didn't interfere. How different it was, or so her mother used to say, from the old tenements, where apparently everyone knew each other and helped each other. And before that, too, when they had lived in the Highlands.

Downstairs, two of the flats were being used as a refuge for battered women. Another two flats on the same landing had been knocked into one big place for the Women's Help office and a public room for meetings. There were all sorts of people living in the building. There were even some immigrants. She'd seen a couple of big black men and one brown-bearded man with a woman in a long robe and her face covered.

Anything could be going on. Every day there was some kind of bedlam or other, the violence a deep hollow echo in bare landings and dark lift shafts.

As she passed her front door, she eyed it anxiously to make sure the security chain was on. Best not to take any chances.

That was what she felt about John as well.

2

Janet Peacock didn't want to leave her lovely big villa in the select area of Bearsden. To think she'd come to this! Especially at her age. She would be sixty-two on her next birthday. She and her husband Charles were members of the local bridge club. They were both regular attenders of the church. Charles was an elder and a personal friend of the minister. She was a member of the Churchwomen's Guild. Each member took a regular turn of hosting a coffee morning. She was always complimented on her home-baked fruit scones and carrot cake.

Charles was a company director, a member of the golf club and much admired for his skill at bridge. He was a popular man and a generous host. His guests could always be sure that at any dinner in his home, he would regale them with a good vintage wine and an excellent malt whisky.

Janet wanted to continue with the normal routine of her life. She wanted to keep her regular appointment with Sharon, the local hairdresser, who could always create such a beautifully neat chignon at the nape of her neck. Then there was the dress shop in 'the village', as the main shopping centre in Bearsden was affectionately called. Miss Peters took such an interest in making sure Janet was well suited. Both Sharon and Miss Peters always greeted her with a welcoming smile and respectful 'Good morning, Mrs Peacock' or 'Good afternoon, Mrs Peacock'.

It was the same in her favourite tearoom. She always enjoyed a rest and a cup of tea before tackling the long walk back home. She had her four-wheeled shopping trolley, of course. It was much easier and more dignified pushing that before her as she walked along, a good support too. She didn't feel fit enough to carry a shopping basket. Indeed, she was hardly fit enough to do anything now. She ached so much. To all appearances, she seemed perfectly all right. She was well dressed and with a good felt hat covering her grey hair. Underneath her smart clothes, however, her body was discoloured with bruises and throbbing with pain. Behind her dignified expression was abject fear. She was in a constant state of tension thinking of her husband's return from his office in Glasgow or from one of his business trips. It was such a blessed relief when he went away for a few days, sometimes for a few weeks.

She had never stopped trying to please him and to avoid, in any way she could think of, his physical and verbal abuse. She knew now that it didn't matter what she did or did not do or what she said or did not say. He would still verbally torment her and then physically abuse her. It had been going on for years. Not all the time. As well as being charming to other people, he could be charming to her, mostly when other people were present, of course. But she never knew what mood he would be in and his vicious moods were getting worse and more frequent.

She could never fathom why he behaved as he did. Did he hate her because she'd never been able to give him a son and heir? Did he despise her because her fear of him had weakened her constitution? She had long ago developed a slight stutter in his company, even when there were other people there. Her memory sometimes deserted her too. Her mind could go blank with fear – especially if she made a mistake at bridge. On such occasions, he would be patient with her. Everyone admired him for his patience and gentleness. Only she knew what he would be like afterwards when they were alone.

No one would believe her if she told them. Of that she was quite sure. They would not even think it was one of her 'little nervous attacks' that she admitted having from time to time. They would think she'd gone mad.

Now, despite not wanting to leave her lovely home and all the special amenities of such a good area, she wasn't able to continue living with Charles. She couldn't stand the pain or the fear any longer. The problem was she had no money so where could she go? How could she keep herself?

Then one day, she saw a programme about battered women and a telephone number went up on the screen. It was the number of 'Women's Help' where, it was said, help and advice would be given in complete confidence to any woman who phoned.

So desperate had she become that, one day after Charles had gone to work, leaving her almost unconscious after an unbearable beating, she lifted the phone and dialled the number. The sympathetic voice at the other end, and the fact that she was being believed, made Janet break down and weep uncontrollably. Years of secret unshed tears rushed and tumbled down her quivering cheeks. All she could manage was, 'I'm so sorry.'

The voice at the other end of the phone kept gently repeating, 'It's all right. Everything's going to be all right. We can help you. Would you mind telling me where you live?'

'Bearsden.'

'All right, I'll give you your local East Dunbartonshire number and you can phone them. They have a twenty-four-hour helpline and, if you phone, you can speak to them. Or if you'd like to speak to someone in person, you can do that too.'

'I need to get away from here. I can't stand it any longer. But I've no money and I don't know where to go.'

'If you phone the East Dunbartonshire number, they'll be able to give you all the help you need. Have you a pen or pencil handy?'

'Yes.'

'Good. Just write this number down.'

Janet copied the number on to the notepad that always sat beside the phone. Within minutes, she had phoned that number and was told what she should do if she decided on the option of leaving.

'Put everything you might need into a suitcase. Also put your birth certificate and marriage certificate, pension book and medical card into your handbag. Then phone for a taxi.'

'I don't have money for a taxi.'

'Don't worry. Take the taxi to this office address, and we'll pay the driver when the taxi arrives. Once you're here, we'll let you know what options you have.'

Janet's hand trembled so much, she had difficulty in dialling the taxi number. She was terrified that Charles might appear before she had got everything packed into two quite roomy suitcases and had succeeded in escaping. She didn't know how she managed it but she did. Within half an hour, she was in the office and a pleasant woman called Elsie was making her a cup of tea.

'Now, no one is going to tell you what you should or should not do, Janet. But rest assured, no matter what you decide, you'll have our total support.'

'I just want to be somewhere safe where my husband won't find me. I know it sounds silly but I'm frightened.'

'No, it doesn't sound silly, Janet, and don't worry. We have places of refuge, safe homes at secret addresses.'

'Oh please, can I go to one of them?'

'There's not always one available but, as it happens, there is one today. You can go to it now, if you don't mind sharing with another woman.'

'No, no – as long as I'm safe and he can't find me.'

'All right. I'll tell Betty and she can take you to the refuge. She's been here at a meeting today but her office is at the refuge you'll be going to.'

Betty, a tall, firm-fleshed woman much younger than Janet, was introduced and in no time they were outside and Betty's strong arms were helping Janet into her car. She was trembling and shivering, hardly able to credit what she was doing. Everything seemed to be happening so quickly.

Was this really sixty-one-year-old Mrs Janet Peacock of Azalea Avenue, Bearsden, stumbling into a car in such an undignified manner? Was she really going away, she knew not where, with a complete stranger?

She felt confused as well as frightened. A few minutes passed before she was able to find her voice and ask, 'Where are we going?'

'Have you ever been in a high-rise building?'

'No.'

'Well, that's where you'll be staying – for a while at least. Until we find you a council house of your own somewhere. But no one will hurry you. We just want you to feel relaxed and safe until you decide what you want to do next.'

A council house? Janet couldn't help feeling shocked. Not that she had anything against people who lived in council houses, she hastily assured herself. But she had never been used to anything like that. She had been brought up in a large bungalow with a loft conversion in a good area. She had gone to a private school. The best private school in Glasgow, her mother always insisted proudly.

'It might not be as posh as Bearsden,' Betty was saying, 'but you'll find the flat has a magnificent view. And there's a park across the road and plenty of buses to and from the city centre. And Springburn's just down the hill. Do you know Springburn?'

Janet shook her head.

'Or Balornock?'

Another shake of the head.

'Och well, never mind.' Betty gave her a reassuring smile. 'You'll soon get to know the place.'

Janet's heart was beating faster by the minute. Her only comfort was the thought that she was escaping from Charles. She clung desperately to the thought.

'Mary McFee is the woman you'll be sharing the flat with. A nice wee soul. You'll like her.'

The name worried Janet.

'Where is she from?'

'The Gorbals.'

The Gorbals? Janet now felt not only shocked but horrified. She had read about the Gorbals and the dreadfully rough people who lived there.

What on earth was she getting herself into?

3

John Ingram was proud of the fact that, in his thirty-nine years, he never showed anger. He had felt anger often enough and never more so than since getting to know Angela. The bitch had led him on, encouraged him at every turn, promised herself on a plate, then refused to follow through. He had kept his cool. She was not going to get the better of him. She had tormented him. He had trusted her, confided his deepest, strongest feelings to her and she had thrown them back in his face.

He had kept his cool. He had been as quiet and as gentle as a kitten. That did not mean she was going to get away with it. Oh no! She thought she was not going to see him? How wrong could she be? Oh yes, lady, you'll be seeing me, all right. Only she wasn't a lady. Cheap, lying, devious slut. They were all like that. The streets were hotching with the little madams, their bellies and half their bums bared for anyone to gawp at. She thought she was getting away with it. Making a fool of him. Taking him for a sucker. That's what she thought but he'd find her. He was clever.

Already he'd picked up clues. Once it had slipped out in conversation that she was 'going across to the park to do some sunbathing'. Then she tormented him by describing how she would strip off to her bikini and lie there alone on the grass.

12

Going across to the park, was she? Going to lie alone, was she? He'd see about that. Already he was working on it. He had made a list of as many parks in Glasgow as he could think of and was hell-bent on searching every inch of every one.

He was also studying nearby houses, houses that were situated 'across' from a park. More recently, she'd let slip (after some of his crafty questioning) that she couldn't see the trees for part of the buildings opposite. Could that mean very high buildings? He became quite excited. High-rise flats? Tower blocks? There were plenty of those in Glasgow. He made another list. He was a patient man. He'd get her all right.

Of course, it might not be high-rise buildings. A hurricane of anger hit him as he realised the enormity of his task. He controlled it. Turned it into ice. After all, he had plenty of time to concentrate on finding her. He'd get her all right.

Hatreds from the past seeped back to strengthen his resolve. It was his revenge, in a way, for all that he'd suffered in the past, his whole life in fact. He'd kept hoping that everything would turn out all right. He wanted to feel safe and happy and, most of all, loved. Always had. But first of all his mother had deserted him. Just walked out one day, left him alone in the house and never came back. He'd been put into care. Care? He couldn't bear to think of the bloody woman who had been coining money for supposedly caring for him. He still had the scars to show for her so-called caring!

Then there had been a few tentative approaches to girls that had come to nothing. They always seemed so much stronger, more confident, than him. How happy he'd been when at last he'd found someone who seemed to satisfy his desperate search for love and security. He had been over the moon. She was beautiful and she didn't seem to mind his long gangly body in comparison. She had the extra attraction of a foreign accent and what to him seemed a tantalisingly mysterious background. They made great plans to visit her home country as soon as they could after they were married. But it had all come to nothing. He soon discovered that she had only married him for British citizenship. She had no desire or intention of ever setting foot in her native country again. She'd used him. She'd seen him as a good catch as well, of course. A successful businessman, albeit in a small way. He had a barber's shop. Men could come into his shop and not be bothered by women. He employed only men to cut and shave his all-male clientele.

There was a growing trend, however, for women hairdressers to tempt men into their fancy salons to sit beside women customers and get fancy cuts. Women were ruining his business, as well as his private life. Not long after their marriage, his so-called wife disappeared. The same as his mother had done. Just walked out one day and never came back.

For no reason at all, except selfishness. She'd suited herself at every turn. Got what she could out of him. That was what this telephone woman was doing. Angela, she was called but she was no angel.

Why didn't she agree to meet him? That was the crux of the whole thing. Her continuing refusal made it quite obvious that all she wanted was to squeeze as much money out of him as possible and for as long as possible.

In his search to find Angela, he went first of all to the Botanic Gardens. He wandered through it and around it. On the Great Western Road side, there was a hotel and some terraced houses. From them, the park was perfectly visible. It was the same along Queen Margaret Drive. Even looking down from Botanic Crescent. Slowly, carefully, he made his way all round the streets – stopping in front of houses and staring towards the park. Eventually he crossed the Botanic Gardens off his list.

Queen's Park was his next destination. Yet again he was frustrated. After a long walk, he found nothing that fitted what he was looking for. This was not the place. His frustration and exhaustion fuelled his anger. He hated the telephone bitch more than he'd hated anyone or anything before in his life. When he found her – and he would find her – he'd kill her.

He arrived home footsore and furious. He collapsed into a chair. Then, after he had recovered his self-control, he lifted the telephone. Her soft voice with its unusual lilt was soon tormenting him again. He kept his cool. Smooth as syrup, his voice was. He asked her casually, 'Been across at the park today?'

'No, I took the bus into town and bought some sexy underwear . . .'

She proceeded to describe the strapless satin bra and thong and all her other intimate purchases.

'So you haven't a car?' He managed to get a word in eventually.

'No, I don't drive. But it's never been a problem. The bus stop's just across the road.'

'And just as handy coming back too, I suppose?' he said casually.

'Oh yes, there's a stop outside.'

So, a bus stop across the road in front of the building that blocked her view of the park and a bus stop exactly in front of her building. He was getting there, slowly but surely. He laughed.

'And of course, you hadn't a heavy load of shopping to lug up the stairs. Only lightweight satin stuff.'

'Och, there's a lift, so I'd be all right anyway,' she laughed in response. Stupid cow. Now he knew it was a high-rise building and she lived high up. And if she lived high up and couldn't see the park for the buildings opposite, the chances were the buildings opposite were high-rise too.

Now, that meant he really *was* getting somewhere. There would only be a few buildings with parks nearby which would meet such exact criteria. He began to feel excited.

Maybe only one.

4

Mabel enjoyed a trip into town to Marks & Spencer's. It was her special treat every week. Eyes flickering down, she left the safety of the house into the bleak brown square of a landing, scratched and chalked with graffiti. She glanced nervously around at the other flats before scuttling into the lift. She felt relieved that no riotous youths had burst from behind any of the doors. This had happened before and, although they ignored her and perhaps didn't mean her any harm, she had felt vulnerable and frightened.

The lift plummeted down. Every time it stopped, men, women and children crammed in. The men could not have come from inside one of the refuge flats because she'd heard that no men, not even fathers and brothers, were ever allowed access to any refuge. Plunging down and down. Doors clanging open and shut. Falling, sinking again. Then at long last she was escaping into the entrance hall. She saw the concierge's office. She caught a glimpse of the green uniform of the concierge as she hurried past. Out now, buffeted by the usual flurry of wind.

By the time she reached the bus stop across the road, she was shivering with the cold air beating around her. Here, because of being on Balgray Hill, she could see the magnificent view through the space between the buildings. She could see green hills and the sparkle of the river in the distance.

The bus came and she struggled on, her bus pass ready in her hand to show to the driver. Before she returned it to her handbag, she checked its date. It wouldn't be long until she had to apply for a new one. That meant the nuisance of having another photo taken. She sighed as she looked at the photo. She had never been attractive. Her mother and father had not been able to hide their disappointment in her. They were both tall and handsome. And there she was, small and skinny with thick pebble glasses. She'd always had to wear them, even as a young child. Now well past retirement age, she had a stoop and, because of her arthritis, had to walk with the help of a stick. Once her hair had been mousy brown but at least it had been thick. Now it was grey and so thin that her pink scalp shone through it in places.

Her mother and father had been ashamed of her. They never said so, of course, but she had always keenly felt their disappointment and shame. She had tried to make up for everything else by being good. She was a very good little girl. They had to admit that. Quiet, obedient, always ready to help in the house or by running errands. Later, when first her mother had become ill and then her father, she was a conscientious nurse and carer.

So good, so helpful, so desperately conscientious that she never had time for a life of her own. Never in her whole life had she even had a friend. She realised now that her mother and father were such a devoted and happily married couple, they had no need of friends or anyone else but each other. As far as their only daughter was concerned, they were totally selfish. Instead of encouraging her to get out and have a life of her own, they believed it was her duty to dedicate herself to them. They took her for granted. The only crumb of praise they occasionally threw in her direction was, 'You're such a *good* girl.'

Well, she was fed up being bloody good. She was going to make up for lost time by being as *bad* as she could. Better late than never. Now she was being bloody bad and making money into the bargain. If only they knew. A bitter surge of laughter choked in her throat. She swallowed it down.

They hadn't even left her any money. She had nothing but her old age pension. Or at least, that's all she would have if it wasn't for John and his regular and lengthy phone calls. She still put up with some calls from other men but they never lasted long.

She was giving John value for money, of course. Nightly sexual excitement for one thing. But much more than that. She was being a good and sympathetic listener. She was comforting him when he needed comfort. An affection had grown between them, friendship even. He had said as much. It was one of the many reasons he had given in trying to persuade her to meet him, go with him for a meal or to a show.

If she had been the person he thought she was, the shapely young woman with the long blonde hair and short skirts, she would have met him. It would have been wonderfully exciting to have met him and gone out with him. If only she could. She felt sorry for him. He pleaded so desperately, yet so gently. She had begun to feel quite desperate herself. She longed to be tall and beautiful with long, blonde hair and a shapely curvaceous body. She still felt a young woman inside. It was only her outside shell of a body that had grown old. The young woman inside her longed to have the sex with John that they so often acted out together. She felt guilty for deceiving him.

In an effort to dispel her guilt, she kept assuring herself, kept repeating to herself, 'I give John value for money. I do all I can for him in the circumstances.'

Every evening she tried to pleasure him in every way she could imagine.

Suddenly she was jerked back to the present by the bus driver shouting at her, 'Is it a round trip ye're after today, auld yin?'

They had arrived at the Buchanan Bus Station and everyone else had left the bus.

'Och, I must have dozed off. I'm so sorry.' Clutching at her stick, she struggled up.

'It's one of them zimmer things ye're needing, hen.'

He got out of his driver's seat and half lifted her off the bus. She smiled up at him.

'You're very kind.'

'Och, I've an old granny at home. I'm well used to this.'

She made her way slowly out of the bus station, past the tall silver sculpture of huge running legs topped with a round white clock in a silver square. She passed one big hotel, then another. It always amazed her how many hotels there were in Glasgow. There seemed to be no end to the building of them. She supposed it must be a sign of prosperity. Across the road was the big concert hall. She passed it, then, turning on to West Nile Street, she braced herself for the wind that always gusted down there. Once she got round on to Sauchiehall Street, she could relax and feel steadier on her feet.

She tutted to herself as she passed all the shops selling cheap T-shirts and miniskirts. Everything was geared for young people nowadays. Across the road was the shop with a windowful of ridiculously skimpy satin underwear. It had been from that window she had gathered her information about the underwear she'd described to John. Long gone were the days when Sauchiehall Street was high class, with beautiful shops where everything had been good quality and in good taste and the assistants were respectful and called every customer 'Modom'.

At least Marks & Spencer's had not changed all that much. She didn't need to buy clothes now. She had enough to last her out. But oh, she did enjoy Marks & Spencer's food. She hobbled about the food aisles with the help of her stick. She enjoyed the sight of the many tasty-looking dishes so much. In the past she could only look and dream but now she could treat herself. Now she had money to buy not only tasty chicken dishes but delicious puddings and even fancy cakes as well.

Thanks to John.

If only things had been different. Poor John. They could never meet and he would never understand.

She had one of Marks & Spencer's special bags that kept the frozen foods cool. She filled it with her purchases and made her way slowly back to the bus station.

The wind tugged at her when she reached her destination on the Balgray Hill and crossed the road to The Heights. Then, just as she got through the entrance door, the tall Women's Help worker struggled past, lugging two large suitcases. She was followed by an elegant-looking, grey-haired woman in a lavender costume and matching hat with a side feather. It reminded Mabel of the outfit the Queen had worn at the first opening of the Scottish Parliament. The woman wasn't unlike the Queen, in dignity at least.

Oh dear, Mabel thought. She won't fit in here. Especially in the women's refuge. She didn't look as if she'd been battered. But apparently men of higher social class made sure the results of their battering weren't seen. They never aimed at the woman's face. She'd seen a programme all about it on television and she'd read articles in the newspapers. It seemed incredible but only too true that it wasn't only drunken working-class men who were abusers. There were far more people like judges, lawyers, doctors, psychiatrists, company directors, policemen and even ministers of religion. It was all a question of manipulation, power and the abuse of power, apparently.

As she stood in the lift beside the Women's Help worker and her companion, Mabel wondered what this woman's husband was – apart from an abuser. Despite her dignified bearing, the poor soul's eyes were brimming with fear and apprehension.

Men could be right beasts, absolute monsters.

Except her John, of course.

5

'If you don't do something about him, Mammy,' Cheryl Patterson said, 'I will.'

Her mother, shoulders hunched in misery, twisted thin fingers on her lap.

'What can you do, hen? I know you mean well and I appreciate it. I really do. But you know what he's like.'

'Yes, Mammy. I know what he's like. He's a hopeless drunk.'

'Och now, he's been all right with you, and me as well. It's just he takes a good drink.'

'There's nothing good about it. He spends all his wages. And you're worrying yourself into an early grave with debt. I'm telling you, Mammy, if you don't get rid of him, he'll be the death of you.'

'Get rid of him?' Mrs Patterson's eyes widened. 'He's my man and he's not a bad soul, Cheryl.'

'Mammy, he's an alcoholic. He could get help if he'd admit it but he doesn't want to admit it. He doesn't want to stop drinking.'

'It's just a wee weakness he has. It's not as if he's ever raised a hand to me. I mean, you can't compare me with some of the poor souls that come and go downstairs. Their men have battered them, nearly killed them.'

'Mammy, he's killing you in his own way. How are you ever supposed to pay the rent? The council would have had us out on the street by now if I hadn't scraped up enough to pay the arrears.'

'I know, hen. You're an absolute gem and I appreciate your help. I really do. I'll try and speak to him.'

'You know fine that won't do a bit of good. You'll have to chuck him out. Lock him out. It's the only way to bring him to his senses.'

'Och, I haven't the heart. He's my man.'

Cheryl rolled her eyes and her mother protested, 'Where could he go, Cheryl?'

'He could go to AA and get himself sorted for a start.'

'All right. I'll speak to him again. I promise.'

'I'm going to have to move out, Mammy. I'm entitled to a life. That's me skint again.'

Mrs Patterson struggled to hold back a panic of tears.

'I don't know what I'd do without you, Cheryl. But you're right. It's not fair on you. Do you think if I spoke to the doctor . . . ?'

'Mammy,' Cheryl groaned. 'It's no use kidding yourself. *I'm* not kidding myself any more. We've spoken to enough folk. Daddy's got to admit to himself what he is and what he needs to do and, as often as not, alcoholics have to hit rock bottom before they do that. Well, I don't know about you but he's not going to drag me down with him. Not any more. Amy Sutherland's renting a flat somewhere near the bus station, I heard. I'm going to ask her mammy where exactly. Maybe I could share with her. If not, I'll look for some place else.'

'Oh, Cheryl . . .'

'And I could get a job in a decent place in town. In one of those big fashion shops, maybe. I could do better than slogging away in that dump of a shopping centre in Springburn.'

Cheryl was getting quite carried away. Her normally pale, creamy skin fired with enthusiasm. Her blue eyes sparkled with pleasure at the imaginary sight of herself swanning about in one of the top-class places in town like Fraser's or Debenham's or John Lewis. Either in one of the fashion departments or in make-up. Yes, make-up, she thought. All the top brands had counters and girls in attendance dressed in smart overalls. The customers sat on a chair in front of the counter while the assistant performed a wee miracle on their faces, chatting all the time in praise of the products they were using. They earned good wages, she'd heard, plus commission on all sales.

John Lewis, right across from the bus station. That would be great.

'I'll tell Daddy you're going to leave us if he doesn't pull himself together. He'll listen then. He's fond of you, hen. He wouldn't want to lose you.'

'Oh yes, he'll say that. And he'll bubble and cry as well. And he'll say he's sorry. And he'll change. And he'll never touch another drop. I've heard it all before, Mammy, and so have you.'

'But maybe . . .'

'No maybes about it. I'm sorry, Mammy. I've had enough.'

Mrs Patterson was trembling now but still managing to imprison her tears. She nodded. 'Of course. You're quite right, hen. You deserve a better life than this. I've been lucky I've had you here for this long. And I'm sorry for taking money off you. It wasn't right. One day I'll try and pay back everything I owe you.'

'Don't be daft.' Cheryl went over and briefly hugged an arm around her mother's shoulders. 'You don't owe me anything. And even if I do get a flat, it's not as if we'll never see each other again. We can meet up in town and I'll treat you to a nice tea in a posh restaurant. How about that? And you can visit me as often as you like. As long as you don't bring Daddy,' she added, her voice acquiring an anxious note. 'In fact, promise me that you'd never even let on where I am. I don't want him turning up drunk and giving me a showing-up.'

'It's terrible sad,' her mother said. 'You used to be that fond of him when you were wee. Remember how he used to take you over to the park and help you catch minnows in the pond and push you on the swings and give you surprise presents? Drink's a terrible thing.'

'Yes, well . . .'

'Remember that time you fell and hurt yourself and he ran all the way with you in his arms to Stobhill Hospital?'

'Mammy, what's the use of looking back all the time? It doesn't do a bit of good.'

'But he's still the same good man . . .'

Cheryl went across the room to stare out of the window. She was struggling to control the impatience that was threatening to spill over into anger.

'I'm still fond of him. He's my dad. And I know he's a good man in many ways but he's an alcoholic, Mammy. I can't help him any more, and neither can you. Nothing's going to change my mind now. I'm going to start looking for a place on my own, or to share with somebody, anybody.'

The room with its bare brown linoleum and sagging moquette sofa and chairs felt depressing and claustrophobic. Everything else had been sold to raise cash, even the television. Cheryl couldn't invite a friend home, either a girl or a boyfriend. She was too embarrassed. Apart from the bare, dismal look of the place, there was always the danger of her father staggering in and making a fool of himself. Or doing something disgusting. Once when she'd had a friend in, he'd thrown up, spewed all over the place – including over her friend's new sleeveless blouse with the big frill down the front.

She could have died right there and then. It was so terrible. That friend quickly disappeared and never came back. She had passed the word around as well. It was the talk of the place. Until something worse happened. He'd peed in the lift. There had been three or four other folk in it at the time. There had been a warning from the concierge after that. Other folk could 'take a good drink' but still behave themselves and 'not act like an animal'.

'I'm not having it,' the concierge warned. 'Maybe other folk can put up with it but I've a job to do.'

Cheryl knew what he meant. Most of the residents just minded their own business. There could be all sorts of things happening, including fights but nobody sent for the police. 'None of my business' was the usual comment delivered by neighbours.

She felt desperately sorry for her mother and had tried as much as she could to help her. However, she truly could not go on being in her present nightmare situation. She got on all right at her work. The problem was she so seldom could go out with the other girls to the clubs or any place at all to have a good time after work. For one thing, she hadn't enough money. Nearly all of her wages went into the house.

She longed for new clothes. All she had was one old denim skirt, one pair of jeans, a couple of shirts and a boob tube. She longed to let her hair down and have a laugh and dance the hours away. She longed to have a boyfriend and a bit of loving.

Fat chance of that. She couldn't even afford decent make-up. Angry and bitter now, she turned away from the window and said, 'I'm away across to the park for a breath of air.'

'Aye, OK, hen. On you go. I'll be all right and it's such a nice day.'

Cheryl picked up her handbag, dug into it for her powder compact – the cheapest she could get from Woolworth's. Rubbish it was. She peered angrily into it as she rubbed a powder puff over her face. She could be quite good-looking, given half a chance, she thought. She had a flawless complexion, not like some of the other girls in the shop. One had a face covered in acne. Another girl was horribly fat, whereas she had a nice, slim but curvaceous body and shapely legs. She had natural hair colouring as well, not like most of the girls, who spent a fortune on hair dyes. Her hair in fact was her best feature – long and glossy and golden blonde.

6

'You can relax here, Janet. This is your home from now on,' Betty Martin said firmly, 'until we can fix you up with a more permanent place. But the wheels of the Housing Department are slow in turning so, meantime, my advice is just relax and try to feel at home here. You're safe, that's the main thing, isn't it?'

Janet nodded. It was all she could do. She was speechless. Everything was so awful. Outside there had been groups of guffawing youths, lads in baggy denims hanging from their bottoms like hammocks. It was as if the trousers were going to drop to the ground at any moment. They wore thin jackets, some with black hoods up that framed pinched, impertinent faces. Others had hoods down revealing hair stuck up in spikes, dyed orange or gaudy green.

Girls were also hanging about in noisy groups wearing shockingly brief skirts and revealing bare midriffs. Some had hair short and spiky and as garishly coloured as the males.

Janet had never seen such awful people. Young people in Azalea Avenue, Bearsden, never looked like that. They either went to boarding school and were never seen at all or they attended local private schools and wore respectable uniforms.

The place was as ugly as the residents. The tower block was one of several, looming high in the sky and creating unwelcoming, icy blasts of wind. It had been warm and calm and quiet in Azalea Avenue.

She found the entrance hall as bleak and as shabby as the outside of the building. She caught a glimpse, through an open door at one side of the hall, of a man with a moustache in a green council uniform. He was crouched over a desk stuffing his mouth with what looked like one of those disgusting hamburger things. A steaming mug sat in front of him.

'That's the concierge's office,' Betty explained as she led Janet into the lift. 'Monty, his name is. He's a really good worker. Very conscientious.'

The lift stank of stale sweat. And was it cats? Surely they didn't allow animals in a place like this. It wasn't even fit for animals. Janet lost count of how many stops and starts the lift made. It seemed to fly upwards forever.

'We're on the twenty-third floor,' Betty said and was soon ushering Janet out and striding across the dark-brown painted landing. There were several doors, one of which Betty opened with a key. Once inside, she dumped Janet's suitcases behind the door.

'This is our office. It's two flats knocked into one. I'll show you around here first and give you a key to your safe house. It's across the landing. Anybody at home?' she shouted, as they made their way along the lobby. The floor of the lobby was covered with lilac tiles that looked like rubber. The place was still and silent except for echoes of noise seeping in from the landing outside.

'Dorothy must be out on a job,' Betty said. 'You can meet her later on. She's officially the children's worker. But we muck in and help each other as much as we can.'

One room had a dark green wall and three lilac walls. It was furnished as a sitting room with a green sofa and two green chairs. There was a coffee table and a standard lamp with a cream fringed top. Another room, with green and lilac walls also, was crammed with two desks, a filing cabinet and office chairs. A place no bigger than one of Janet's cupboards in Bearsden was crammed with two blue easy chairs and a coffee table. It was used, Betty explained, as a counselling room.

Then there was a big room which had originally been two rooms, Betty told Janet, but a dividing wall had been knocked down. This could be used for meetings and various things like English classes for immigrants and a play place for residents' children. There were pieces of paper stuck all over the lilac-painted wall. Lilac and green were obviously the favourite colours in the place. It wasn't until later that Janet discovered they were the colours of the suffragette movement.

'The colours of the brave souls who fought and died for women to have the right to vote,' Betty told her. Now Betty indicated the papers pinned to the wall. 'By the immigrants practising their English writing.'

Janet noticed a couple of papers ending with 'I love English. I love my English teacher.'

Toys filled one corner – a teddy, a Barbie doll, building bricks, a pedal car, a toy cooker with little pots and pans, a board game and a pile of gaudy coloured picture books.

Back in the lobby, Betty flung open another door. 'The bathroom, the kitchen, a couple of cupboards. Now we'll go across to the refuge you'll be staying in. Here's your key. Wee Mary, your flatmate, has one and there's one kept in the office but we always ring the bell first and give a shout to let the occupants know it's only us. We don't want to give anyone a fright just walking in.'

Betty rang the bell and called through the letter box. 'It's only me, Mary.' There was a shout of 'Come in'. Then Betty opened the door and led Janet into a long lobby similar in shape and colour to the one they'd just left. A tiny frail-looking woman with a slight stoop and rounded shoulders was standing in the sitting room door. She wore shabby slippers and a wraparound apron. She reminded Janet of her part-time domestic help.

'Hi there,' Betty announced cheerily. 'I've brought a new lady to share the flat with you. Mary, this is Mrs Janet Peacock. Janet, this is Mrs Mary McFee.'

'Gosh!' Mary gazed with some awe at Janet. 'That's a posh name. You look posh as well, hen. Fancy your man knockin' the likes of you about, eh? It just goes to show. Come on in.'

It was on the tip of Janet's tongue to deny any wrongdoing by her husband. She felt not only ashamed but affronted. Nobody had ever known anything about her private life before. At least, not the truth. But of course, everybody would know now. There was no use denying anything. She suddenly felt like crumpling up and weeping. She had put on a respectable front for so long and with so many people. She managed, however, to continue holding her face stiff.

'How do you do,' she said to Mary and proffered a leather-gloved hand.

Mary laughed.

'I feel I should curtsey or something. Fancy a cup of tea, hen? The kettle's been on the boil.'

A cup of tea had always been a great source of comfort.

'Thank you.'

Betty said, 'Right, I'll leave the pair of you to it then.' She had a confident way of talking as well as moving. 'You'll show Janet around, won't you, Mary? And tell her everything she needs to know.'

'Aye, sure.'

'I'll look back later, Janet, and check you've settled in OK.'

'Thank you for everything.'

'Nice big lassie,' Mary said as Betty left them. 'Come on, I'll show you into your room, hen. Where's your stuff? Oh aye, she's left your cases in the lobby. Let me take them in for you. In here, hen.'

Janet noticed that Mary had a bald patch on the back of her mousy brown head. The bald patch awakened frightening memories in Janet, of Charles pulling her across the room by her hair, then punching her breasts until she was gasping for breath and choking with pain. She broke out in a weak sweat at the memory. She had escaped. Yet she still dreaded the thought of his fury when he arrived home. Especially now when he found that she had gone. He'd see that she'd taken everything. Every stitch of clothing and every pair of shoes. (Not that she had a very large wardrobe but what she did have was of the best quality.) She had also taken all her jewellery, some of which was worth quite a lot of money – her mother's watch and brooch and diamond ring, for instance. Janet sank down on the edge of the bed.

Mary patted her on the back. 'Don't worry, hen. You're aw right now. Take your hat and coat off. I'll go and make the tea. Come back through to the living room when you're ready.'

Janet nodded. She sat for the next few minutes trying to calm her breathing. She was in another world, a strange world she had never known, never really believed existed.

'That's me pourin' it oot,' a voice called.

In a daze, Janet removed her hat, automatically patted her hair tidy. Then she took off her coat and laid both hat and coat on the bed. It was a narrow single bed covered with a cream-coloured duvet. There were two single beds in the room. Surely she wasn't expected to share a bedroom with the awful woman?

She found her way through to the living room and sank into one of the dark green easy chairs. Mary handed her a cup of tea and Janet concentrated on keeping her hands steady as she accepted it.

'You'll feel better after you drink that, Janet. Is it aw right to call you Janet?'

Janet nodded. The tea helped and so did the comfort of the deeply cushioned chair and the heat that emanated from the electric bar fire. The floor was covered with lilac linoleum but there was a pink and blue and fawn Chinese-type rug under her feet.

'How large is the flat?' Janet managed at last.

'Well, there's this living room with that dining area.' Mary jerked her head towards an alcove in which sat a table and four wooden chairs. 'There's a decent-sized kitchen, four bedrooms and a bathroom with a shower as well as a bath.'

'Four bedrooms?'

'Aye. One for you and one for me and two others for any other poor souls that need them.'

'There are two beds in my room.'

'Aye well, you might have come with weans. There's a cot in one o' the cupboards and a couple of folding beds as well. Just in case.'

'Goodness.'

'Aye, we're lucky just now wi' just the two of us. But even with a crowd you manage somehow. It's no' easy, mind, but anything's better than what we had to suffer before. And it's just temporary. Ah've been here longer because them wi' weans get priority for council houses, y'see.' Mary turned away her face and gave a sniffle of distress but within seconds she had turned back and was saying cheerily, 'But don't worry, hen. We'll get on like a house on fire. Want another cup?'

'Yes, please.'

Mary poured the tea.

'I put milk and two sugars in. Was that OK?'

'Yes, thank you.'

'I had a right pig of a man,' Mary said, settling down in a chair at the opposite side of the fireplace. 'A right pig. To me, that is. To everybody else, he was Saint Michael. That hard done to – having to put up with me. Long-suffering and patient with me when I took a drink. What everybody didnae know was he drove me to drink. He never thought I was good enough for him. Nagged away at me all the time. Put me down. Made my life a misery. Rotten, two-faced swine.'

Mary has her Saint Michael, I have my Saint Charles, Janet thought and was moved to say, 'I know exactly what you mean.' Her voice acquired a bitter twist. 'Oh yes, exactly.'

'He took my weans as well.' Although Mary's voice remained defiant, she gave another sniffle of distress.

'Oh, I am sorry.'

'His mother moved in. She never thought I was good enough either. Treated me like dirt, the pair of them. They shut me out eventually. Without even a coat on my back. I wouldn't have cared but it was the weans.' She took a big gulp of tea. 'They wouldnae let me have my weans. OK, I'd been out for a wee refreshment but, as I say, that pair would drive anybody to drink. Auld harridan his mother is. Never out of the church, though. Saint Michael and Holy Jeannie. I didnae stand a chance. But I'm no' going to give up fighting for my weans. The Women's Help lassies are getting me a lawyer and they're going to help me to get a place of my own for when I get my weans back. How about you, hen?'

The situation once more struck Janet as unbelievable. It was just too awful.

'I'd rather not say. If you don't mind,' she added, trying to be dignified but not unfriendly. After all, this poor woman didn't want to be here either. Although, by the look of her, she would probably not be too unfamiliar with a tower block area like this. Or a tenement building in some sort of working-class area.

'No, I don't mind, Janet. I know how you must be feeling, hen. Come on, I'll show you around and where everything is kept in the kitchen.' Her slippers flopped on the floor as she went along the lobby and into the kitchen.

'We take turns of cleaning the house and we each cook for ourselves. We have our own wee bit of cupboard and fridge shelf to keep our own food in. You'll no' feel like nippin' out for anything today so you can have a share of mine for tonight. And I've plenty cornflakes and bread to do us both for breakfast.'

'You're very kind.'

'Us girls need to stick together, hen. If you don't fancy going down the road for your messages, there's a bus stop across the road and plenty of buses to take you into town. There's a nice park as well across the road. Lovely inside, so it is. You'll enjoy a wee walk in that park. You'll be OK here once you find your way around, believe me. I mean, I'd be as happy as a lark here, if I just had ma weans.'

Janet followed the drooping, shuffling figure into the kitchen and was relieved to see that as well as being fitted out in as modern a style as her own kitchen in Bearsden, it was spotlessly clean. In the bedroom, Mary guided her across to the window.

'Would you look at that view, hen. Isn't that something, eh?'

Indeed it was. Janet couldn't help admiring it and she experienced – for the first time, if only for a few seconds – a joyous sense of release. Here, from her situation in the sky and stretching for miles below and far beyond like a jewel in the sun, was the city of Glasgow. It was nestling serenely in a distant, magic circle of shimmering lochs and hills. She had never seen Glasgow, or thought of it, in such a way before.

'Magic, isn't it?' Mary said as if reading her thoughts.

'Yes indeed.'

But when Janet turned back into the room, her nightmare immediately returned and, with it, her feelings of confused unreality. It was now late afternoon. She should be preparing dinner for Charles. His key would be turning in the door at any minute. Everything had to be exactly right for him, even down to the way his cutlery was set on the table. And his napkin. The meal had to be exactly at the right temperature, as well as having the right taste. Not too much seasoning. Or too little. The whole procedure was an agony of anxiety and suspense.

Janet could see an alarm clock on the bedside table. Any minute now. Her legs gave way and she sat down on the bed.

'Are you all right, hen?'

'I was just remembering,' Janet said faintly.

'Och, try not to worry, hen.' Mary sat down on the bed beside her and put an arm around her shoulders. 'He'll no' get you in here. By jove, he'd better no' try or he'll have me to deal wi'. I'll protect you, hen. Kick him up the arse, so I will.'

Janet couldn't help a half-laugh, half-sob escaping. It was so ridiculous really. This undersized woman, with her bad posture and her drink problem, was so common. She was not the type of person Janet would normally allow anywhere near her, never mind touch her. But nothing was normal any more.

'You're very kind.'

'And you're beginning to sound like a broken gramophone record, hen.'

Another weak laugh escaped and, all at once, Janet was grateful for wee Mary's arm around her shoulders.

7

Glasgow Green was not only the oldest park in the city but the oldest in Britain. In 1450, James II granted the Green to Bishop William Turnbull. Bishop Turnbull gifted the common lands of Glasgow Green to the people of Glasgow. It was bordered by the River Clyde and the Gorbals to the south, Saltmarket and the High Court to the west and the Calton and Bridgeton districts to the north and east. Public executions took place on the Green up until 1865. Many's the time John Ingram had visited the Green, strolling under the impressive McLellan Arch, designed by Robert and James Adam, and past Nelson's Monument, erected by public subscription and the first monument in Britain to be erected in Viscount Horatio Nelson's honour. There had long been a Glasgow insult of 'He'll die facing the monument', because the worst criminals always used to be hanged outside the High Court and facing Nelson's Monument.

For years, Ingram had enjoyed the different events that took place on the Green. In his youth, it was the Football Centre and the place where the heavy horses were stabled and exercised. Later there was the World Pipe Band Championship and annual fireworks display. Not to mention the pop concerts, funfairs, local events, like rowing regattas, and charity events, like the Great Scottish Run.

There had been a great deal of building all round the area including, most importantly for his purpose, high-rise flats.

He'd left the shop in the care of the three barbers – one middle-aged man and two younger men – he had been employing for quite a long time and knew were dependable. He had been staying off work a lot recently because of his continuing search of all the parks. Not that the men seemed to mind. They were probably quite glad not to have the boss breathing down their necks all the time.

He found a few possible buildings in the Glasgow Green area and hung around them all morning before going back into the Green and the People's Palace, a museum devoted to the social and cultural history of Glasgow. At the rear of the building were the Winter Gardens, a massive glass conservatory filled with shrubs and flowers. There he had lunch in the café under the glass roof among the hothouse plants.

Then it was out again for the afternoon to stalk the houses and the rest of the park. All the time he fingered the cut-throat razor in his jacket pocket, a relic from his father's day in the barber's shop. He'd give Angela another chance to be decent and make it up to him. He had just wanted to meet her and allow their relationship to develop naturally. He kept trying to explain to her over the phone. She always sounded so sympathetic and understanding. So why, oh why, did she keep refusing him? That's what he wanted to know, needed to know. He realised that it must be just the money but he didn't want to believe it. After all, the money didn't amount to all that much. It wasn't as if she was making a fortune out of him.

And surely there was one decent, loyal and loving woman in the world. He had thought he had found her in Angela. He wanted it to be her. He wanted it so much that he could hardly credit her stubborn and evasive attitude to his perfectly reasonable requests. He had assured her they could meet in a busy public place if it was nervousness that was holding her back. It would be her choice. He would go along with anything and everything she said. What more could he do?

Well, he knew what to do now if she continued to refuse his simple and reasonable request. He would track her down. He could and would find her – even if it took him weeks, months, years. He could be as stubborn as she was. No, far more than stubborn. Dedicated.

Angela, he must accept whether he wanted to or not, was selfish and money-grubbing. She had betrayed his trust. He had been such a trusting fool, opening his heart to her and making himself vulnerable. How could she be so cruel? What had he done to deserve such treatment? When his wife had betrayed him, he'd kept asking himself the same heartbroken question. His emotions kept seesawing between the same desolation, longing and wild hatred.

He stood for a few minutes, staring around. A couple of young women appeared and stood nearby. Their attention was on the huge building of Templeton's carpet factory. Or at least it had once been a carpet factory. Now it operated as the Templeton Business Centre. There had been a terrible fight way back in the eighteen hundreds to stop the factory being built in case it spoiled the appearance of the Green. Eventually permission had been gained for a building modelled on the Doge's Palace in Venice. Now there it still stood, an exotic assortment of coloured brick, with circular and pointed windows.

The girls were admiring it. One of them had blonde hair. But it was cropped short and he could hear her American accent. She was reading from a guidebook. 'And the façade collapsed on 1st November 1889, killing twenty-nine women and girls.'

He wandered about, hands dug deep into his pockets, watching every woman he came cross. Or at least, blonde women. Angela had told him her long fair hair was her best feature. He saw one girl with hair that answered the description but she was only a child, skipping along, holding on to her mother's hand.

His own hair was black as night and straight with a long lock that kept sliding down to shadow one side of his face, no matter how often he smoothed it back. He was tall and lanky. Angela said she liked tall, slim men. He wasn't good-looking, he'd told her. His eyes were too small and deep-set, his nose too long and his lips too thin. Angela said she thought men with deep-set eyes and thin lips were sexy. She had built up his self-confidence. Only to undermine it again.

He felt sick and tired, depressed too, and frustrated to the point of tears. He suddenly began loping towards the monument in an effort to release his frustration. Once in the Saltmarket, he sped past the Justiciary Courts with their Greek-columned façade until, becoming out of breath, he was forced to slow his pace again. Head moving forwards and backwards over his long neck with its protruding Adam's apple, he looked like a featherless crane as he forced his legs to keep pacing along until he reached a bus stop. He caught a bus to take him to Bearsden Cross. He had a nice big flat there above his shop in the nearby Drymen Road.

Obviously it had not been good enough for his wife, though. Not even Bearsden was good enough. If she'd confessed, explained to him why she'd married him, he maybe could have found it in his heart to forgive her. Maybe they could have worked something out. But no. Just like Angela, there was no explanation for rejecting him. Well, his wife maybe got off scot-free but Angela was not going to. Oh no!

In the sitting room, a clock weakly tick-tocked through the heavy silence. The hall and the sitting room had wood-panelled walls. He had once been proud of the panelling. He'd had the job done (at great expense) by a local joiner after he'd seen pictures of panelled walls in stately homes.

He'd thought it would impress his new wife and she would feel proud too.

Now the walls depressed him. They made the place look dark, lonely and abandoned – like himself. He sank his long, lean frame into a chair and lifted the phone.

'Angela?'

'John.' There was the usual lift of pleasure in her voice. 'How are you?'

'Lonely.'

'Never mind, dear. I'll soon cheer you up.'

'No.'

'Darling, you know that I can always make you feel loved and happy.'

'No.'

'Oh dear, you are in a strange mood tonight.'

'If we could just meet. I keep telling you that if you feel a bit nervous, we could . . .'

'No, definitely not.'

'But why not?'

'Trust me. It's impossible.'

'But why?' he repeated.

'Darling.' Her voice acquired its sexy purr. 'Just relax and listen.'

At first he had enjoyed the way her soft Highland voice could thrill and excite him. Now it was a torment that hardened his bitterness into hatred.

'What are you wearing?' he cut in at one point.

'Something new. It's called a boob tube. It stretches tight over my breasts and leaves my shoulders and arms bare. It's bright red in colour . . .'

He could vividly imagine how she must look in that. She had so often described her big breasts. Sitting hunched alone in the dark room, he could have wept.

'I need to see you,' he said without hope. 'Just to see you.'

Ignoring his plea, as he knew she would, she continued to torment him.

He managed a calm 'Goodnight' eventually, without betraying a hint of his seething anger. He went through to the bathroom and splashed cold water on his face. The cold water didn't help. He wanted to go out again and search for her but he was too exhausted.

In the kitchen he took one of the local bakery's sandwiches from the fridge and returned to his chair to eat it without knowing what it tasted like. He couldn't concentrate on anything except his plans to find Angela. He couldn't even sleep for thinking about her and what he was going to do to her. He writhed about in bed and was glad to get up early and go downstairs to open the shop. He had everything set up and ready by the time his three employees arrived.

Dave, the oldest, had a spare set of keys and he said, 'I could have opened up, Mr Ingram. How's your Aunty? A bit better, is she?'

'What?' For a moment, Ingram didn't know what the man was talking about. Then he remembered he'd told the men that he had to go and see to an old aunt who was ill and lived alone. 'Oh, she's still pretty poorly. I'll have to go back again today. Are you sure you'll manage OK, Dave?'

'No bother. Don't worry, we're managing fine. But here, you missed a rare bit of gossip.'

'Did I?' he murmured absently.

'Yes. Old Mr Cameron was in for his short back and sides.'

'Enough said.'

Mr Cameron was well known as a right old woman. Any titbit of gossip and he was in his element.

'Nothing juicy surely? Not in Bearsden.'

'Juicy enough. You know Mr Peacock?'

'He's not done anything shocking,' Ingram said. 'I don't believe it.'

'His wife's done a runner.'

'No! Not Janet Peacock! Run off with someone else?'

Despite his wayward thoughts, Ingram's interest was awakened.

'No, of course not. She's ancient.'

'Not that ancient. He's in his sixties and she could be a year or two younger than him.'

'Would you fall for a woman of that age?'

'Definitely not but she's maybe gone off with another old guy.'

'What they're saying is, she must have gone off her head. She takes funny turns, apparently. They'll probably lock her up in some loony bin when they find her.'

'She must be mad, leaving a man like that and a place like that. He's obviously loaded. But that's women for you.' Ingram's mouth betrayed a twist of bitterness. 'There's no telling what they'll do or why they do it.'

The shop door bell tinged and a customer entered. Ingram said, 'Can I leave you boys to it then?'

'Sure. Away you go, Mr Ingram,' Dave said. 'We'll manage fine.'

Out on the main Drymen Road, he walked along to the bus stop and caught a bus into town without knowing where he would go after reaching the centre of the city. All he knew was that parking a car was hellishly difficult in town. For what he needed to do, it would be easier to take the bus and then walk about. Once in the city centre, he decided to go into the information office in George Square. The place was filled with books about Glasgow and maps and souvenirs. He browsed for a while until he found a book about Glasgow tenements. He also bought a couple of maps. It was a hot day and a few people were relaxing in the seats between the flower beds and the tall grey statues. The magnificent City Chambers dominated the square at the east end, towering over the Cenotaph. It was hard to imagine that originally the square was a grazing ground for sheep. Once it had been a favourite place for drowning cats and dogs and slaughtering horses.

By lunch time, office workers, students and tourists were packing the square, many eating sandwiches and drinking coffee from the baker's across the road. The pigeons were mobbing the ground in front of each seat, pecking and jostling for crumbs. Ingram interrupted his reading to purchase a sandwich.

The book he'd bought was all about the redevelopment of Glasgow housing and how, because Glasgow in the nineteenth century was in the throes of industrial and commercial expansion, its working-class housing had an immediate need for growth. The tenements at the centre of the old city around the High Street and Saltmarket had fallen into decay and demolition work there and in the adjoining areas such as Townhead and Calton had begun.

There were pictures of the outside of slum tenements and the cramped conditions of the inside of some of them.

There were pictures of Swedish timber houses and aluminium bungalows that replaced the slums in some districts. Then came the development of the high-rise blocks of flats. His attention sharpened. He read that within months of completion, blocks of twenty or thirty storeys made teeming microcosms of places like Cowcaddens or Garngad. The Red Road blocks, because of the number of children and inadequate lift provision, created a blight of juvenile delinquency. Some blocks in Springburn and on the Balgray Hill had 'deck access' and were the focus of a variety of vandalism problems. The quarter-mile decks or corridors were also found by young tearaways to be ideal for motorcycle races.

He'd forgotten about Springburn and Springburn Park. He was almost choking with excitement as he opened the coloured maps. Yes, here it was and there, in front of the park, were several blocks of high-rise flats with a road in between. He would bet his life that there would be a bus stop immediately outside one of them.

8

Cheryl's mother had got a job as a cleaner in Stobhill Hospital and was able to repay some of the money she'd borrowed from Cheryl for the rent arrears.

'I don't want it back, Mammy,' Cheryl said. She knew that her mother was doing everything she could to stop her from leaving. 'And you're not fit enough to be cleaning in Stobhill, or anywhere else.'

'Your daddy hasn't had a drink for over a week now, hen. He's really trying his best. He was that upset when I told him you were thinking of leaving and it was because of him. He said he was sorry and . . .'

'I know, I know, he told me. He promised he'd never touch a drop again.'

'He gave me all his wages – except for a few pounds he needed for cigarettes. It was such a help and what with my wages as well as your daddy's, we'll soon be able to pay you back the rest of the arrears money.'

'I told you, Mammy, I don't want it back.'

In fact she was very glad to get it back. She could at last treat herself to something to wear, something really fashionable. Already she was looking forward to having a good browse around the shops. So far there hadn't been any luck in finding a flat to rent, or rather, one to share, because rent nowadays, at least for private flats, was ridiculously high. Especially if it was in a decent district like the West End. She'd always wanted to live in the West End. Lots of young people lived there, students mostly or actors and actresses and writers – interesting people. That was because of the BBC and the university being in the area. She would love to have gone to the university.

Apart from anything else, it was such an impressive building with its Flemish spire soaring up from the top of Gilmorehill. Once she'd mingled with the crowds of young men and women students, meaning to follow them into the building but, at the last minute, she lost her nerve. Instead, she'd just stood at the big iron gates wistfully watching them.

She might have become one of those students. After all, she'd done well at school. But of course she could never have afforded to go to university. Her mother needed her to go out and find a job as quickly as possible and earn some money.

'Away you go and treat yourself to something nice, hen,' her mother said now. 'You deserve it. No, don't you touch the dishes. I'll do the washing up.'

'Och, you must be dead beat, Mammy. I'm worried about you having to work in Stobhill. It's far too much for you.'

'I'm fine, hen. Honestly. I'm that pleased and happy that your daddy's all right now.'

'Oh Mammy!' Cheryl groaned. But it was no use saying any more. Her mother was a born optimist. At least as far as her husband was concerned. He was on back shift this week and the pubs would be shut by the time he finished work on the railway, so he wouldn't have the chance to drink. Cheryl felt sure, however, that come his change of shift next week, it would be a different matter.

She finished work at half past five but most of the shops in town were open until eight, sometimes nine o'clock at night.

She would have plenty of time, not only to window-shop but to actually buy something.

'Are you sure?' she asked her mother.

'Yes, away you go, hen. Enjoy yourself for a change. Go to the pictures as well or one of them disco places, eh?'

'Maybe another night, once I've got something new to wear.'

'Anything you say, hen. Be as late as you like. You've got your own key.'

It was pathetic how eager her mother was to please her and make her feel she didn't need to leave home. She felt sorry for the older woman and gave her an impulsive hug before leaving.

Going down on the lift, she met a woman from one of the refuge flats. Alice Donaldson, her name was. Alice was not much older than herself, a pretty girl with fair curly hair. They'd chatted a few times on the lift and recently they'd bumped into each other in town and had gone for coffee. It was on that occasion Alice told her what had brought her to the refuge. Her husband had been physically violent and the last time when she'd been pregnant, he'd punched her so viciously on her stomach that she'd lost the baby. It was while she was in hospital she'd contacted the Women's Help number on her mobile phone. She'd gone to the office in town as soon as she was able. She'd immediately been introduced to Betty.

'Betty, God bless her,' Alice said, 'took me to the flat and has kept her eye on me and helped me at every turn since. She's taken me to the Housing Department and my name's on the waiting list for a house of my own now. I don't know what I'd have done without her.'

'Your husband doesn't know where you are?' Cheryl asked.

'No and I hope to God he never finds out.'

At least, Cheryl thought, her father had never been violent, had never once 'lifted his hand', as her mother said, to either of them. Maybe there was hope for him yet.

They emerged together from the lift into the entrance hall. A couple of children were throwing stones at the concierge, who dashed out to chase them. They were too quick for him, however, and he turned back as the girls reached the street.

'Don't even belong to this block,' he growled. 'Evil wee devils. I'll throttle the pair of them if I get my hands on them.'

'I'm going into town to see if I can get something new to wear,' Cheryl told Alice. 'Fancy coming with me?'

Alice hesitated.

'If it was earlier in the day, while he was at work, but I'm terrified he'd be on the loose at night and see me. I'd die with fright.'

'Another time then?'

'Yes, thanks, Cheryl. I'd love to. I'm just popping down to the local shops. I've run out of porridge and I love it for my breakfast.'

'See you.'

Cheryl gave her a cheery wave before sprinting across the street to the bus stop. A bus was coming along and she swung on to it. She felt quite optimistic. OK, Amy Sutherland had already got a tenant to share her flat but there would be other chances, other flats. Meantime, she'd just enjoy her wee bit extra money.

She was free. There was no man to bother her and make her life a misery. Not like poor frightened Alice, anyway, and the other girl she shared the refuge flat with. Well, not so much a girl. Black-haired, dark-eyed, Rita was in her thirties and had two young children. It couldn't be easy for Alice stuck in the same flat along with someone else, especially someone with children. The children, a boy of five and a girl of seven, were nervous wee souls and clung to their mother.

It was an awful job to get them to school. Alice said Rita had to drag them there every morning and be at the school gate every playtime to reassure them. Then she had to be waiting there when school finished to collect them and see them safely back. They absolutely refused to go out to play and there were such great places across in the park. God knows what they'd all suffered before escaping to the refuge.

Dorothy, the children's worker, said not to worry, the children would be all right. She'd got some lovely toys and games for them to play with in the playroom. If she wasn't around, Betty, the other Women's Help girl, would play with them or read them stories. Cheryl could see how they were becoming all right. At least they trusted Betty and Dorothy. Dorothy especially was great with them. Her normally sad face would change completely with her dimpled grin and daft antics to make the children laugh. They had gone over to the park with Dorothy recently, holding tightly on to her hand all the time but still . . .

'They obviously feel safe with the girls and no wonder,' Alice said. 'Talk about angels? I don't know about the new woman – Janet, I think her name is – but wee Mary and Rita and me love those girls. We hate to see them go off duty at night and don't feel really safe until they come back next morning. Then we all relax again. It maybe sounds daft to you, Cheryl, but it's the truth. That's how we all feel.'

Cheryl didn't think it was daft at all, although she couldn't help feeling a bit amused. The Women's Help girls were the most unlikely-looking angels. Betty was tall and well-made with straight auburn hair that she had a habit of tossing defiantly back. Dorothy was small and thin, with blonde hair tied neatly at the nape of her neck. The two of them had other things in common, though. They were both caring and hard-working. They not only cleaned the office and meeting room in their place but they also cleaned the flats each time a woman was rehoused and had the flat all clean and fresh in time for the next woman arriving.

'What would we have done without them?' Alice had said.

Apparently there were refuges all over the country. Were there no happy marriages, Cheryl began to wonder? It was enough to put anyone off men, although she still nursed romantic dreams of meeting some handsome young guy who would think she was marvellous and treat her like a queen. The local talent wasn't much use. Most of them had already been banged up, graduating from borstal-type detention centres to Barlinnie Prison. A lot of them were into drugs. If it wasn't drugs, it was drink. She wanted none of it.

Once in the town, she walked along Sauchiehall Street, then down the hill of Buchanan Street. Buchanan Street always made her feel happy and exhilarated. It was a really great street. Especially on a Saturday. At the top end, there was the big Concert Hall building with an enormous screen perched high up on the roof. In front of the building and leading up to it was a half-circle of a couple of dozen or more steps. Sitting on the steps was a rainbow of brightly dressed young people. At one side, a trumpet player was blowing his hardest and swinging energetically around.

Looking down the hill, Cheryl enjoyed the sight of the great swarm of people milling about. A few small tables were dotted here and there. They were draped with slogans, one against the Iraqi war, one against the Israeli conflict, one against cruelty to animals. Young people at each table were handing out leaflets. Further down, two men with moustaches in cowboy boots and big hats with the brims turned up at each side were strumming guitars and belting out 'Cigarettes and whiskey and wild, wild women . . .'. Further down again, about six or eight young men and girls in scarlet T-shirts were enthusiastically bouncing up and down and banging on different sizes of drums. The noise was terrific. Cheryl felt excited and was tempted to jump up and down herself. Down near the Argyle Street end, a man resplendent in a full Highland outfit was adding to the cacophony of noise with the bagpipes. It always reminded Cheryl of how much she loved Glasgow. And how loving Glasgow was loving life.

Cheryl decided not to go into Princes Square shopping centre. It was known as Buchanan Street's 'jewel in the crown'. It had once been an enclosed courtyard. Now it was an elegantly glass-roofed and multi-floored shopping mall. Its shops were exclusive and chic, with lots of designer label clothes.

Not my scene, Cheryl thought. I've a bit more money just now but not *that* much. It maybe wasn't quite as pricey as the Italian Centre in Ingram Street with its Armani and Versace but it was still too pricey for her.

She crossed over Argyle Street to St Enoch Square and went into the St Enoch Centre. She enjoyed herself wandering in and out of the shops there. A pair of high wedge-heeled sandals looked and felt good when she tried them on and so she bought them. Then a lovely white linen trouser suit caught her attention and she couldn't resist it. She could just imagine wearing it with her bright red, figure-flattering boob tube. A flimsy white scarf decorated with pink hearts was her final purchase.

She walked on air back up Buchanan Street, then ran to the bus station to catch the bus home. Getting off the bus, she saw her father trudging up the Balgray Hill. Not staggering and taking up the whole width of the pavement but walking neat and straight. It was at times like this when he was sober that she couldn't help loving him. He was a slightly built man with thick grey hair under his railway cap. His hands were stuck in his overall pockets until he saw her and gave her an eager wave.

'Hello, hen.'

'Hello, Daddy.'

He linked arms with her as they entered the building.

'If I wasn't so tired, I'd take you for a walk in the park. It's such a grand night.'

'I haven't the energy either. I've been trudging around the shops.'

'A young lassie like you. That shouldn't be any bother.'

'I've been on my feet all day down in Springburn, remember.'

'Aye, right enough. We're lucky having such a nice park so near, though. Mind we used to catch minnows in the pond? And I played footie with some of the lads.'

'Uh-huh.'

They had to squeeze into the lift and they nodded to some of the occupants, only recognising them by sight as being neighbours. Once they got into the house, her mother greeted them both with a kiss and then wanted to find out what was in Cheryl's shopping bag. Cheryl could see that her mother had a struggle not to show her disapproval of the purchases.

Looking at the sandals, she murmured worriedly, 'Will you no' fall over in them, Cheryl? I mean with such thick soles and high heels?'

Of the white suit, she asked, 'Will that no' get awful quick dirty, hen? That's a lovely wee scarf,' she added hastily.

Cheryl laughed and took the things through to her room. She could hear the water splashing in the bathroom as her father tried to wash away some of the railway grease and grime before sitting down to his supper. He worked hard and her mother used to say, 'He deserves a wee drink after a hard day's work.'

She didn't say that any more because the trouble was it was never a wee drink. It was a bucketful. He didn't seem to know, or to be able, to stop once he started.

'I got fish suppers. Is that all right, hen?' her mother asked with the note of anxiety that her voice never seemed free from these days.

'Great, Mammy. Thanks.'

Her earlier happiness still clung to Cheryl. Life wasn't so bad after all.

9

Springburn Park was a forest of evergreen and flowering trees, riotous rhododendrons, heathers and alpine plants. It had one of the most beautiful rockeries in Scotland, a garden of peace and three wildlife ponds. The peace garden was beautifully laid out with heather beds, memorial seats, pergolas and a 'Peace Pole' donated by Japanese atomic bomb survivors.

Alice Donaldson sat on one of the seats. It was good to escape from the flat for a time and get some peace. Rita's children were on holiday from school and were in a squabbling mood. She could understand it and sympathised with Rita and the children. The children were frightened to go out in case their violent father saw them. Rita shared their fear and couldn't hide it. She tried, of course, for the children's sake and her voice could be bright and she'd say things like, 'Don't be silly. Daddy can't find us here. Daddy's away in Aberdeen. Miles and miles away.'

As she said the words, sometimes even with a scoffing laugh, Alice could see – and she was sure the children could also see – the haunted look of fear in Rita's eyes. Alice discovered one day when she'd been chatting to Rita on her own that her husband was a commercial traveller and could be anywhere, any time, including Springburn and Balornock. When she'd asked Rita what her marriage had been like and how her husband had treated her and the children, Rita struggled in silence for a moment or two and then shook her head.

'I can't bear to talk about it, Alice. It's too awful. He was really disgusting – the things he did to me . . .'

She began to tremble violently and Alice became quite upset herself at the sight of Rita's distress.

'I'm so sorry, Rita. I shouldn't have asked. Try to forget about him. You're safe now. That's the main thing.'

'That's what Betty and Dorothy keep telling me and I try to feel safe. But I can never quite manage it. It's a nightmare that'll always be with me.'

'I know it's a well-worn cliché, Rita, nonetheless it's true that time heals. It's been proved over and over again.'

Alice also pointed out that the children were getting better – showing little bits of improvement.

'Look how they can stay with Dorothy when you need to go out shopping or to the doctor's since they've been off school.' The problem was in the evenings once Dorothy and Betty went off duty. They were all stuck in the flat together night after night in the close proximity of the small sitting room. It wasn't the children's noise or bickering that was the problem for Alice. It was the ache that she suffered in the company of any youngsters. She had always longed so much to have children of her own. Now, because of her husband, she could never have any. Paul had injured her so badly . . . Her eyes and mind closed at the thought. She couldn't bear it.

She had come, this summer evening, to sit in the Garden of Peace to see if the beauty of the place might ease the pain in her heart.

To think that she had loved Paul once. She had loved him for a long time and she had tried so hard to please him. She thought he'd loved her too. He'd told her often enough. He'd said as a loving married couple, they didn't need anyone except each other. He'd made it seem that she was hurting him or insulting him if she had any contact with anyone else. Gradually she was persuaded to drop all her friends. She could see now that he was purposely isolating her. It was all right for him. He was at work all day mixing with other men and probably women too in his office. She was alone all day, feeling lonely and depressed. Then he began criticising her, humiliating her, belittling her, undermining her self-confidence. Then mental torture turned to physical abuse as soon as he found she'd become pregnant.

Since she'd been in the refuge, she found that this was quite a common pattern.

'It's the universal language of abuse,' Betty said, tossing back her glossy mane of hair, her features hardening. 'It's men wanting power over their partners and to control them and manipulate them.'

Sometimes she said it was mental and emotional abuse without the physical side and that was just as painful and unendurable.

With a sigh, Alice got up from the seat and left the garden, hands stuck in the pockets of her blue gilet. In an effort to take her mind off these sad thoughts, she concentrated on admiring everything as she walked along. The extensive woodland and greenery was alive and cheerful with robins, blue tits, chaffinches and wrens. In one pond she passed, she saw water fowl. There was a heron near another. In yet another, there were mute swans, coots, moorhen, mallards, little grebe and tufted ducks nesting in the islands. She sighted a roe deer. Soon she found herself in a clearing called the 'kickabout area'. There was a football match going on and quite a crowd had gathered to watch it and cheer on their side.

Suddenly, to her horror, Alice caught sight of a familiar face. It was Mr Clarke, their next-door neighbour from Pollokshaws. He had seen her, was actually waving to her. Often he chatted to Paul over the garden fence. He was a widower and, she guessed, a bit lonely and glad of a talk while both he and Paul were out working in their gardens. She used to take a cold beer out for each of them. But of course she knew she daren't relax and stand and talk with them.

Mr Clarke was coming eagerly towards her. She turned away as if she hadn't noticed him and began retracing her steps, quickly, until she was running through the trees and on to the Balgray Hill and across to her building. Her heart was hammering in her chest. Her mind was in a chaos of panic. She didn't know how she got into the lift, up to the twenty-third floor and out onto the landing. The dismal graffiti-covered landing looked threatening now. Her fingers fumbled frantically in her jacket for the door key. When she found it, it slipped through her violently shaking fingers and clattered on to the floor. Sobbing now, she hammered on the door.

'It's me, Rita. Open the door.'

The door opened cautiously but Alice pushed at it and almost knocked Rita over in her haste to get inside, bang the door shut again and put on the chain.

'What's wrong,' Rita cried out, 'and where's your key?'

'Oh God, I've dropped it outside.'

'On the street?'

'No, just outside the door.'

'Go and sit down. I'll get it and bring it through to you.'

Weakly Alice did as she was told and was collapsed back in one of the easy chairs when Rita came into the room and dropped the key on to her lap.

'I've just made a pot of tea and you look as if you need a cup.'

'Thanks, Rita.'

Rita had been washing her black hair and it clung wetly to her scalp, making her face look not just thin but gaunt. In a matter of minutes, she had brought the cups and poured out the tea. After they each had a few sips, Rita said, 'What on earth got you into such a state? Did you see your husband? Did he see you?'

'Just as bad. Our next-door neighbour. He's sure to tell Paul.'

'Where? Inside the building?'

'No, in the park.'

'Well, that doesn't mean he knows where you live. He didn't follow you, did he?'

Alice's face twisted with anxiety. 'I don't think so. I ran in among the trees and I didn't look back. He might have. Oh God, I hope not.'

'The chances are you'd know the park better than him. Within a couple of minutes, you'd be out of his sight among the trees. You'd be away from the park, across the road and into the building before he'd even got his bearings. Don't worry, Alice. Relax and drink up your tea. Take one of your sleeping tablets and have an early night. Then in the morning you can talk to Betty about it. I'm sure she'll say the same. Nobody's going to find you up here. And they'd never let any man into the house, that's for sure.'

Alice nodded. Rita thought again how young Alice looked and how pretty she was, with her crown of blonde curls. In this state, she seemed even prettier with her gaze wide and appealing and her skin flushed rosy pink. She hoped for both their sakes that what she'd just said was true. That no men would be allowed in the house and they'd be safe.

'The children asleep?'

'Yes, I managed to get them down early, thank goodness. They were tired out wandering about all day with Dorothy. They've got me exhausted now. We borrowed a ball from the playroom and went over to the park for a so-called game of football earlier on.'

The mention of football brought the scene of the football match vividly into Alice's mind again. She wished with all her heart that she'd looked back to see if Mr Clarke had followed her. Even if he hadn't, Paul would very soon know that she must live in the Balgray Hill area. Admittedly, the Balgray Hill wasn't the only side of the park. It was also bounded by Broomfield Road and Balornock Road. He would know, however, that she couldn't afford to live in those other roads. It was common knowledge that some high-rise buildings were favourite places for the Housing Department to put people like herself. In her particular building, there certainly were plenty of people who had some problem or another. Some were unemployed and on the dole. Some were immigrants. Some were known as 'problem families'. From what she could see of the youths hanging about the place, they were problems all right. Then of course there were the refuges, or 'safe houses'. She didn't feel very safe right now.

'Forget it,' Rita urged. 'Will I switch on the TV? Maybe that would help take your mind off it.'

'What did we do,' Alice asked, 'to deserve the life we had, Rita?'

'We didn't *do* anything. How many times do the girls have to tell you? You mustn't blame yourself. Your husband was a selfish, power-mad control freak. A right manipulative bastard. He would have acted the same to you even if you had been an angel straight from heaven. It wasn't your fault, Alice. Any more than what my dirty pervert of a husband did to me was my fault.'

Alice sighed.

'It's just, I wish it could have been different. I loved him and, before we were married, he was so nice . . .'

'I'll bet. So was mine. A good laugh as well. The life and soul of the party. All the women thought he was great. Still do, I expect. If only they knew.'

'Do you know the best thing about here?' Alice suddenly asked.

'We're safe.'

'That too but it's the fact that people like Betty and Dorothy *believe* us, are one hundred per cent on our side. *It's being believed!*'

Rita had begun to blow-dry her wet hair.

'How about if I ask Dorothy if she'll look after the kids tomorrow and you and I give ourselves a treat to cheer ourselves up? Go to the pictures maybe? Or a wander round the shops and a cup of tea in a nice restaurant. I've never been to that Willow Tearoom above the jeweller's in Sauchiehall Street. Have you?'

'No but I'm all unnerved.'

'I don't blame you but I was just thinking, it would help us both if we could get out and keep our minds occupied with other things. We're not helping ourselves sitting cooped up here in misery. That's letting the bastards win.'

'But will you be all right, Rita?' Alice knew only too well that Rita was also afraid to venture far from the safe house.

Rita said, 'Hopefully, if we stick together, we should be all right. Even if, God forbid, one or other of the bastards did see us, they wouldn't give themselves a showing up in front of anyone else.'

Rita had a point. That and the hot sweet cup of tea were beginning to make Alice feel more optimistic.

'Right enough. Mr Clarke wouldn't know what direction I'd taken once I was in among the trees. And there's so many houses for miles all around the park.'

'And people from all over Glasgow visit Springburn Park. Even people from further away than Glasgow. You could have been living in Edinburgh or anywhere and just through in Glasgow for the day.'

As usual, when any of the women tried to support each other, they began to get quite carried away.

Hope sprang eternal.

10

'This is your new flatmate, Mrs Sandra Elliot,' Betty announced to Janet and Mary.

Janet said, 'How do you do' and proffered her hand to the apprehensive-looking girl with brown hair and wide eyes staring up from a fringe of hair hanging over her brow.

Mary said, 'Hello, hen. Don't worry. You'll be aw right wi' us. And Betty's a wee gem.'

'Not very wee,' Betty laughed. 'But who cares?'

'No' us anyway, hen. You can look the size of an elephant and you'll still be a wee angel to us. Isn't that right, Janet?'

Janet smiled. Mary's common speech and manners still embarrassed her but she'd come to realise that Mary was, nevertheless, a good-hearted person and had certainly been kind to her.

'Yes, Betty is very supportive to us all.'

'Here, I'm away before my head gets too big for my hat.' Betty laughed again. 'The pair of you make yourselves useful and show Sandra around. I'll see you tomorrow morning when I come back on duty, Sandra. Don't worry, you're going to be fine.'

After Betty left, Mary said, 'Sit down, hen. Make yourself at home.'

'Perhaps we should show Sandra her room first,' Janet ventured.

'Oh aye, right enough. Well, you do that, Janet, and I'll make us a bite to eat. OK?'

'Very well, just follow me, Sandra. Is it all right if we call you Sandra?'

Sandra nodded. She looked very young, in her early twenties at most.

'Here we are. As you can see, it is a pleasant, comfortable room. And do please have a look at the view. Isn't that magnificent?'

Sandra nodded again.

'Where is your luggage, dear?' Janet enquired, adding gently, 'Or did you not manage to bring any?'

Suddenly Sandra's young face overflowed with tears. Janet took her into her arms and patted the girl's heaving shoulders.

'Now, now, it doesn't matter. Betty will see to all that. We look after each other here. You'll get used to it. It's very different for me too, being in such a place. I came from a lovely villa in Bearsden but I have settled in now and so will you. Indeed, I'm grateful to have found the place. It's so helpful. Every other Friday, for instance, Betty and Dorothy organise a get-together for a cup of tea and a chat with the other women across the landing and also some women who have left here and are happily settled in a house of their own. They were safe here and were able to grow stronger and then move on. It is so reassuring to meet them and talk with them. This place is well named, believe me, as a refuge.'

'Is it really safe?'

'Absolutely, rest assured. I personally would have preferred the flat to have been situated in a quieter, more respectable building. Nevertheless, one gets used to the riff-raff element outside and one just ignores what's happening on the other floors. In here, we are all right, we understand each other's problems. We help each other and we are safe.'

'Thank you, thank you for being so kind.'

'Tuts, I have done nothing. Come now and enjoy a cup of tea with us. You'll begin to feel a bit better after that. By the way, Mary always has her own pot of tea at her elbow. She's a terrible tea jenny. She stews tea and drinks it all day.' Janet shuddered. 'It must taste vile.'

As Janet thought, the tea helped Sandra to calm down.

'Fancy the bastard battering a frail wee lassie like you!' Mary said, topping up her cup from her brown striped teapot. 'See men!'

'He was so different before we were married. I really loved him and I thought he loved me.' Her brown eyes widened. 'I wonder if I disappointed him in some way and that's why he changed.'

Mary said, 'He did batter you, didn't he?'

Sandra nodded. 'I had to hide in cupboards or up in the loft. It was the drugs, you see. He started taking drugs. Then after a while, if he couldn't get any, he went absolutely mad.'

'Aw, a druggie?' Mary groaned. 'They'd batter their granny to get enough cash to feed their habit.'

'I believed everything he said at first but now I can't trust anything he says and I never know what crazy thing he might do. He's got worse and worse and the last time, I sent for the police. He was arrested. He'll never forgive me for that. If he finds me, he'll kill me.'

She was beginning to tense up again and stare apprehensively up from under her fringe.

'He won't find you, don't worry. But I can understand how you feel,' Janet said. 'We all go through the same, feeling frightened we'll be found, I mean. But it's never happened. Betty says she's been in the job for many years and it's only happened once, ages and ages ago, and it wasn't here. It was up in Luss, I think she said. Some little village anyway, years and years ago. They got rid of the man without any problem. The police saw to that and the woman got an interdict – I think that's some sort of restraining order – put on him. They moved the woman to another place as well. But that was just one case in years and it wasn't here. Nothing ever happens here, Betty says.'

'I hope she's right.'

'Try and relax,' Janet soothed. 'You're perfectly safe now. Have a piece of cake. It's from Marks & Spencer's. They have such good quality food, I always say.'

'It's so sad because before he started on drugs, you couldn't meet a nicer man.'

'Och aye,' Mary's tone was sarcastic, 'I'll believe you, hen.'

They had another cup of tea and Sandra began to visibly relax as they chatted together. Later she helped set the table for supper once she was shown where everything was kept.

'We all do our own shopping and make our own meals, usually,' Janet explained. 'We each have our own food cupboard and shelf in the fridge-freezer. It's a big fridge-freezer so there's plenty of room. And don't worry, you can have a share of my macaroni cheese tonight.'

'And my porridge in the morning, hen. And if you don't feel able, I'll get your messages tomorrow. Have you got any cash at all?'

'Yes, the Women's Help office advised me to put money aside and have my marriage certificate and birth certificate and health insurance and medical card, all that kind of thing, kept handy. That was before I plucked up courage to leave but I knew I would have to make the decision eventually. I got so frightened.'

'You haven't a Glasgow accent, Sandra. Do I detect an Edinburgh one?'

'Yes, I originally belonged to Edinburgh.'

'Such a lovely city.'

'Since my father and mother were killed in a road accident, I've never felt the same about the place. Of course,

I realise the traffic and the roads are just as bad everywhere else.'

'Fancy you losing your mammy and daddy,' Mary said. 'As if that wasn't enough without that bastard making your life hell.'

'Have you no relations?' Janet asked.

'I have a married sister in Edinburgh. Happily married, thank goodness. I didn't want her to be worried by my problems or put in any danger from my husband. So I've never told her. She lived abroad with her husband for a while, of course, so I never had the chance. I'll have to write or phone before long, though, or she'll begin to wonder what's happened.'

'She can come and visit you if you want her to but her man won't be allowed in, hen. It's a strict rule here. No men, not even daddies or grandpas, are allowed over the door. Boys are allowed to stay with their mammies if they're under sixteen but older weans like that aren't allowed any pals in. We've got to know who's who, y'see. There's got to be rules. Everything's for being on the safe side, y'see.'

'Obviously everything's been thought of. That makes me feel a lot better.'

'Oh aye. See Betty and Dorothy. They think of everything. Born for the job, so they are.'

'They have their own problems, of course,' Janet said. 'That is why they are so understanding and sympathetic. They are both divorced, they told me.'

'Aye, that's true. But aw the same, no' everybody with a divorce is as good and hard-working as them two. They haven't even a cleaner. They do everything themselves, so they do. We think oursels lucky, don't we, Janet?'

'Oh yes, indeed we do,' Janet agreed.

'And no' everybody would have bothered about me with my drink problem.'

Sandra looked taken aback.

'You have a drink problem?'

'I'm getting to grips with it. I've never had a drink since you've been here, have I, Janet?'

'No, indeed. You have been very good, Mary. We are all proud of you.'

'Every time I crave a drink now, I just have a wee cup of tea instead.'

'Have you met Alice Donaldson and Rita Jamieson, Sandra?' Janet asked. 'They share the other safe house.'

'No.'

'I expect Betty will introduce you tomorrow. She would want you to get settled in first.'

'Do you think I could borrow some notepaper and an envelope? I'd feel better if I wrote to Patricia right away. Patricia's my sister.'

'I think I might have a notelet left.' Janet rose and went through to her room. In a minute or two she returned. 'I'm afraid it's only a small one. Will that do?'

'Yes, thank you. It's just to let her know where I am. I'll explain everything when I see her.'

Mary said, 'I'll post it for you tomorrow when I'm out for my messages. And if you think you need a sleeping tablet to get you through tonight, hen, I could ask Alice next door. I know she has some.'

'No, thanks. I've got tablets from my doctor. I can take one of them.'

'Aye, OK hen. After you have a bite to eat, you get a good night's sleep. The first night's always the worst, isn't it, Janet?'

'Yes but it does get better. Try not to worry.'

Later, Sandra just picked at the plate of macaroni cheese that Janet put before her. Janet and Mary finished their portions with obvious enjoyment. After the meal, Sandra said, 'I'll do the washing up.'

'No, no,' Mary and Janet cried out in unison. 'You get away to bed. We'll do the dishes.'

Then they were taken aback when Sandra impulsively kissed them both, before disappearing from the room.

'Poor wee soul,' Mary said, starting to gather up the dishes. 'See men!'

Janet shook her head. 'Drug addiction, it seems, is a growing problem. I was reading the other day about the amount of crime that is drug related. Even very young people . . .'

'I worry about my weans. I'm no' there to see what's happening to them.'

'Surely your husband . . .'

'He doesn't care about them. He just kept them to spite me.'

'But at least they're too young to know about drugs, Mary. And both Betty and Dorothy are doing their best to get things sorted out for you.'

'I know. God bless those girls. And please God help them get my weans back,' she added with much feeling.

Janet started putting the milk and sugar dishes and cake plate on to a tray as Mary carried another tray of dirty dishes through to the kitchen.

After putting the milk in the fridge, the sugar in the cupboard and the cake in a cake tin, Janet went back to fold the table cover and put it away. It was then she noticed Mary's teapot on the little side table next to her easy chair by the fire. She wondered if Mary wanted the teapot washed out. She lifted the lid to see if there was any tea left in it. It was then she noticed a peculiar smell. She peered and sniffed closer.

Good gracious! she thought, in sudden distress, Mary had been sitting all day and every day drinking beer, not tea, under their very noses.

She must report this to Betty and Dorothy. It was her duty. No doubt it would mean the end of any attempt to get Mary's children returned to her. It could mean that Mary would be put out of the refuge. She felt affronted at being deceived by Mary but even worse at the thought of Betty and Dorothy being deceived by her.

It was really *awful*!

She was shocked at Mary. Then shocked at herself. Incredibly, a suspicion of laughter was beginning to bubble to the surface of her mind. She was becoming as bad as the awful woman.

II

Mabel stood beside Cheryl as they went up in the lift. She knew she was called Cheryl because another girl standing next to her was calling her that. Cheryl was calling the other girl Alice. Cheryl looked strikingly beautiful in a white trouser suit and a red boob tube. Her golden hair was tied at the nape of her neck with a red ribbon. Mabel had seen her in the red boob tube before but the white suit, she guessed, must be new. She made a mental note to describe it to John. She modelled herself mostly on Cheryl when John asked her to describe herself. It was how she would have liked to be. All her life she'd dreamed of looking as beautiful as Cheryl.

The girl called Alice was pretty too but with short curly hair. She was wearing a fringed denim skirt and a fringed waistcoat over a pale blue T-shirt. Mabel wondered if John would like that outfit. Alice came from one of the refuge houses. Mabel had seen her on a previous occasion there before she entered the lift. Alice was telling Cheryl about a new girl – Sandra, her name was – who'd arrived to share the refuge flat with wee Mary and Janet. Wee Mary had told Alice that Sandra's husband was a druggie and poor Sandra was terrified of him.

'She looks a timid wee soul,' Alice said. 'Betty brought her in to introduce us. She hardly opened her mouth. But wee

Mary said to give her time. She had opened up all right to her and Janet.'

'About as bad as drink,' Cheryl said. 'Alkies and druggies – six and half a dozen.'

'Wee Mary says Sandra's husband sometimes goes berserk, behaves like a madman. Your dad doesn't act like that, does he? He seems a harmless soul to me.'

Cheryl shrugged. 'He's just weak, I suppose. But he causes a lot of harm all the same. I'm looking for a place of my own and, as soon as I find something, I'm away from here.'

Oh dear, Mabel thought, who can I use as a model then? She'd already told John she was fair-haired. Who else was blonde around here? There was this Alice, of course, but her hair was short and curly. She'd told John that her hair was long and straight. And there was Dorothy, the children's worker. Dorothy and Betty, the other worker, were well known in the building. However, Dorothy didn't dress young or trendy. She had nice dimpled features but she often looked sad and tired.

Alice got out of the lift and, after giving Cheryl a quick wave, hurried over to one of the refuge houses. Cheryl and some others stayed on and the lift shot up higher and higher. Mabel's flat was on the twenty-fifth floor. Cheryl must live even higher because she was still standing in the lift when Mabel left.

As soon as she arrived inside her flat, Mabel locked the door and, still using her stick, moved slowly through the long lobby and into the sitting room. She usually managed without her stick in the house because she could take her time, walk carefully and, if necessary, hold on to things. Today, however, she felt tired. She eased herself down on to her chair. It was a warm day and she didn't bother switching on the electric fire. With a sigh she gazed at the worn brown carpet, the large old-fashioned furniture and thick brown plush curtains. She would like to have gutted the whole place. She had always hated her mother's taste in furniture and furnishings. Everything was so heavy and dark and depressing. But she couldn't afford to buy bright modern furniture or anything else for the house. The day might not be far off when she would no longer be able to afford her jaunts into town and her little treats of having morning coffee in Bradford's tearoom. Or afternoon tea in the Willow Tea Rooms in Sauchiehall Street. Or one of her shopping sprees for food in Marks & Spencer's.

Oh, she would miss everything so much. It looked, however, as if no matter how hard she tried to please John, nothing mattered to him now except the chance to meet her. She'd kept trying for as long as she could but her heart was heavy. She knew it was no use.

She heaved herself up and trailed through to the kitchen to make herself a cup of tea. While she was drinking her first cup, she took a tray of cauliflower cheese out of the fridge and put it into the microwave. Thankfully the fridge, the freezer and the microwave had been in the flat when her parents moved in. Otherwise, they would have had no modern conveniences. She sat hunched on a stool in the kitchen and ate her meal without tasting it. She was still thinking of John and how desperately sad and lonely she'd feel without him.

She carried her second cup of tea through to the sitting room and, after drinking it, sat half-dozing, her thick spectacles slipping down to the end of her nose, her gnarled, veined hands resting on her lap. The grandfather clock struck six. The clock had belonged to her mother's family for generations and the ghosts of the long dead still clung to it.

The phone rang as usual, before the clock had stopped chiming.

'Darling John . . .'

'My dearest Angela.'

'How are you tonight, John?'

'Getting sadder and more depressed as each day passes without seeing you.'

'Oh, my dear, why can't we just go on as we've always done? We've been happy, haven't we?'

'Not any more. I can't go on like this indefinitely. There doesn't seem any sense in it.'

For the first time, she detected a hard edge to his normally smooth, gentle voice. In an attempt to delay the inevitable, inescapable end, she said, 'Perhaps one day . . .'

'Soon?'

'We'll see.'

'Why do you keep tormenting me?'

'Oh, I'm so sorry, John. I don't mean to torment you. You mean more to me than anything or anyone else in the world. The last thing I want is to hurt you.'

'Well, then . . .'

'I'll try and arrange something.'

'Soon?'

'My dear, you don't understand. There's complications.'

'Are you married? Is that what it is, Angela? There's another man? Is that the complication?'

'John, I'm awfully tired tonight. Do you mind if we leave it just now?'

Mabel gently, reluctantly, replaced the receiver.

John did the same. He was thinking, so that's what it is. There's another man. All right, I'll soon get him out of the picture. At least he'd found the place. He had gone to Springburn and walked up the Balgray Hill and seen the park. In front of the park, facing each other on opposite sides of Balgrayhill Road, were two rows of high-rise buildings. He did not know which of these tower buildings Angela lived in but he was a patient man. He'd wait and watch every day, even if it took months. He'd wait and watch and he'd find her. One way or another, he'd also find the man and, after he found the man, he would no longer be a complication. He would make sure of that.

He began to feel elated, excited.

Mabel, on the other hand, felt sad. The time was coming. It wouldn't be long now. Oh, how she would miss him.

*****

Sandra Elliot asked wee Mary if she would mind posting the note to her sister in Edinburgh. Sandra was too afraid to go out.

'Aye, no bother, hen. I was going out for my messages anyway. Can I get you anything while I'm in the shops?'

'I don't like bothering you, Mary. I should go myself.'

'Och, don't be daft. You'd help me if I needed it. We all need help at first. I'll get you all you'll need to start off. Milk and sugar and tea and a loaf of bread. And what do you like in the mornings – cereal or porridge?'

'Cornflakes usually but I can't expect you to . . .'

'Be quiet, will you? I'll get a few frozen things as well. We can square up with money later on.'

'I don't know what to say, Mary.'

'Just do as you're told and don't say anything. I'll no' be long.' She turned to Janet. 'Behave yourself, the pair of you, till I get back. Have you everything you need, Janet?'

'Yes, thank you. I managed out to the local shops yesterday.'

'Along the road?'

'No, I took the bus down to Springburn.'

'It's a disgrace what they've done to Springburn.'

Sandra raised an anxious eyebrow. 'What do you mean?'

'Before your time, hen, Springburn used to be a really nice place with lots of great shops. I had an aunty and uncle used to live in Cowlairs Road. It's gone now. At least, I've no' been able to find it.' She sighed. 'Happy days, long before I met my shit of a man. Just a room and kitchen, my aunty had, with the lavvy out on the landing and no hot water in the house. Just one of them swan-necked taps with cold water. I stayed with them after my mammy died. I shared the room bed with five of my cousins.'

'Good gracious!' Janet gasped. 'How awful for you.'

'No' a bit of it,' Mary protested. 'We were as snug as bugs in a rug in that wee house. And my aunty and uncle were as happy as larks. As my aunty used to say – great neighbours, the Co-op on the corner with everything to look after you from the cradle to the grave and Hoey's department store, just to mention a few of the great variety of shops. What more could anybody want, my aunty used to say.'

'Good gracious!' Janet repeated.

'But now,' Mary shook her head. 'What with all these motorways and new buildings, the heart's been taken out o' the old place. I get lost, so I do. My aunty would birl in her grave if she could see it now.'

'Will you be able to carry everything, Mary?' Sandra asked worriedly. 'I feel so guilty but I just can't face venturing out yet.'

'I'm taking my trolley. So stop worrying. You're an awful wee lassie. Always worrying.'

'I know and I admit I was worrying about having nothing in to eat or drink. And of course, it's terribly important to post the note to my sister.'

After Mary had gone, Janet said, 'Mary is a bit . . .' She paused to give Sandra a meaningful look. 'Nevertheless, she has a heart of gold.'

'Yes, I know. She's been so good to me. You both have. And so sympathetic and understanding. I really do appreciate it. I feel ashamed to be such a coward and a nuisance but I can't help it. If you only knew how terrified I am of my husband.'

'My dear, the reason I, for one, can understand how you feel is because I'm just as terrified of my husband. I pray day and night that he'll never find me. I'll die if he finds me. I'll die of terror, I assure you.'

'I'm sorry, Janet. I didn't realise. Is wee Mary the same?'

'I don't think she's afraid of her husband in the same way as we are. What she's terrified of is losing her children. Of never seeing them again.' Janet hesitated. 'By the way, poor Mary has a little drink problem.'

'Yes, she did mention it.'

'Don't ever touch her teapot. She pretends to everyone that it's full of tea but I discovered it's actually beer she's drinking from it all day. I ought to have reported it to the girls but . . . I just couldn't bring myself to do it. I just pretend I don't know and I hope you'll do the same. That's why I'm warning you not to touch her teapot. If you did, she'd be worried then that you knew and would report her. She might get put out or worse, you see.'

'Oh, I'll not touch it or say anything.' Sandra put a hand to her mouth and, for the first time, laughter brightened her brown eyes. 'It's awful but . . .'

'Yes, I know. That's exactly how I feel. What a carry on!'

No doubt Mary would be getting rid of her empty beer cans and renewing her stock of full ones while she was out. Janet had been tempted, at one point, to lecture Mary for her own good but decided that it would be no use. As long as Mary never got drunk, Janet supposed, there would not be too much harm done. If it had been whisky or gin in the teapot, that would have been a different matter.

*****

Up on the thirtieth floor, Cheryl was singing to herself. Something nice had happened. All right, maybe it wasn't a dream come true. Maybe Tommy McKechnie wasn't the handsome young man of her dreams, who would think she was marvellous and treat her like a queen. But he was the nicest guy she'd met so far and he was really interested in her. He had a decent job as a bus driver. He didn't take drugs or bother about drink. He could take an occasional pint, he'd told her, but he'd far rather spend the evening with her having a meal and a glass of wine and then go to the theatre, than go to the pub with the lads.

They had gone to Pizza Parlour and then to the Pavilion. It was a typical Glasgow comedy show and they'd enjoyed a right laugh. Tommy wasn't handsome but he had a nice face and a good head of ginger hair. He hated his hair and the freckles that went with it but she didn't mind at all. Anyway, as she told him, it wasn't all that gingery, more auburn. Quite a nice shade really. And he had only a very faint dusting of freckles across his nose. His eyes were grey-green. He didn't like them either but she told him she liked them and to stop being so hard on himself. He looked cool. She told him that.

She and Tommy had been out together three times now and were getting on great. She liked the way he kissed too. She couldn't take him into the building for a snog. It could be as busy as Buchanan Street. So they'd gone for a walk in the park before saying goodnight outside her building. She had told him that she was looking for a place of her own or to share with someone. He lived with his mum and dad down in Springburn and he said, 'I'm twenty-one years of age now. It's high time I was moving out on my own as well.'

That made Cheryl begin to think and hope that it might become possible to share with Tommy. Why not, after all? She was beginning to feel more cheerful, more hopeful, by the day.

12

'Feeling a bit better now, Sandra?' Betty settled her firm flesh into the cushions of the chair.

Sandra smiled her gratitude. She felt so grateful to Betty, she believed she loved the big woman with the mane of auburn hair. Betty had such a cheerful, confident personality, everybody felt more secure in her presence.

'How can I ever thank you, Betty?'

'What for? I'm just doing my job. By the way, you were saying you had a sister in Edinburgh. Do you fancy staying with her or looking for a flat in Edinburgh? Or if you want, I could find out if there's a vacant place in one of our refuges there.'

'I've written to my sister and asked her to come through and see me so that we can talk things over. I didn't want to try to explain over the phone. It's too complicated. It'll be an awful shock for her once she does find out – that this is a refuge, for a start. She never knew what my husband was like. She and her husband were living abroad for a while.'

'Well, just let me know if and when you decide to go to Edinburgh.'

'I told Mary and Janet I've never been that keen about living in Edinburgh again but I'm too nervous about bumping into my husband in Glasgow now. So, I'm beginning to think that perhaps that might be the most sensible thing.'

'There's no rush. You have a good talk with your sister and then let me know your final decision. She might insist you go and stay with her for a while. But you're welcome to remain here for as long as you feel you need to.'

'Thanks, Betty. By the way, I bumped into Rita this morning. I said it was good to see her wee ones playing happily across the landing with Dorothy. Poor Rita didn't look happy though. She never talks about what she suffered. But it must have been terrible.'

'Hopefully Rita will eventually be able to start a new life for herself.'

'Wee Mary said Rita has counselling sessions with you. Does she open up to you all right? Do you know what happened to her?'

'What goes on and what's talked about between all of you in the safe houses is up to you and the others, Sandra, but what you or any of the others say to me at counselling sessions is strictly confidential.'

Sandra flushed. 'Oh, I forgot. I'm so stupid.'

'No, you are not stupid. You're a very intelligent, sensitive, caring young woman. You keep telling yourself that because it's the truth.'

'Do you think I'll ever get back to normal? Ever be able to go out and about again? Ever be able to get back to work?'

'Of course. You just need time. I've seen it happen so often. Once a woman is completely free of her abuser, it's just a question of time. Usually, with a bit of help, encouragement and support. But there's nothing wrong with that.'

'I used to get on all right at my work. But he kept ridiculing my job and me. I was a nursery school teacher and he used to say things like I was more like one of the kids than one of the teachers. I used to laugh at first. But it got worse until he was really undermining my self-confidence. Then he'd accuse me of things like being unfaithful with one of the male teachers.

The violence came with the drugs. Even the drugs seemed all right at first. Just a social thing, he said. But I think what happened was he progressed from the soft social kind of drugs to the hard addictive ones. Then he'd go mad if he couldn't get a fix. I feel it's so sad because I think we could have worked things out in our marriage if it hadn't been for his drug addiction.'

Betty shrugged.

'Most of the women I've known in this and other refuges have had abusers that didn't use drugs but the abuse started with much the same pattern you've spoken of. They play mind games. They ridicule your job or your beliefs. They humiliate you. They isolate you from workmates, friends and family. They accuse you of all sorts of things, including infidelity. Then there's the physical abuse. Nothing to do with drugs. It's a deliberate choice men make to exercise power and control over their wives or partners.'

'You don't think he turned to drugs because of something inadequate in me?' Sandra ventured timidly. 'Maybe if I had . . .'

'No, I don't. Watch my lips, Sandra. *It was not your fault!* Now I'd better go across and get on with tidying up the office. We're up to our eyeballs in paperwork at the moment.'

Just then Mary appeared in the living room doorway.

'Betty, I saw Rita and the weans going across to the office as I was coming out the lift. But Dorothy's out, isn't she?'

Betty bounced up. 'Never mind, I'm just going across.'

Rita and her little boy and girl were waiting in front of the office door.

'Hello, Rita,' Betty greeted her cheerily as she proceeded to unlock the door. 'Hello, Bobby, hello, Susie. Come on in.'

They were hardly over the threshold when a tragic-eyed Rita announced, 'They've got nits!'

'Och well, that's no big deal. Kids get them all the time.'

'They've never had them before.'

'Never mind. Dorothy's got a fine-tooth comb in the first aid cabinet. We'll soon get rid of the wee blighters.' Betty laughed. 'The nits I mean. Not our wee Bobby and Susie.' She patted their heads. 'I've got a tin of sweeties in my cabinet. Come on, they're your favourites.'

★★★★★

Ingram took the car. Normally he didn't use the car on the few occasions he went into town because of the parking problems. However, he drove up the Balgray Hill and, without any difficulty, found a parking place with a good view of the tower blocks. He sat in the car, shoulders hunched and head pushed forward, long fingers wrapped around the steering wheel. He felt taut with excitement. He saw exactly which high-rise building it must be. There were the bus stops. There was the building facing the park but with the view partially blocked by another tower building. His eyes stayed glued to it. It was called The Heights. She was in there. He knew it. His emotions rocketed about. One moment he was feeling joy at the prospect of seeing her. The next moment fury engulfed him at the thought of her appearing with another man. One moment he was thinking how wonderful it would be if he was able to free her from this 'complication' and have her to himself. The next moment he was hating her for having deceived him for so long.

He had brought a flask of coffee and a box of sandwiches and, after a time, he poured himself a cup of coffee and sipped at the hot liquid without taking his eyes off the building. There was a group of shabby-looking youths standing near the entrance. They looked as if they were on drugs. A couple of young children came skipping along followed by a woman carrying a shopping bag. They disappeared inside.

Old newspapers and other rubbish flapped and flew about in the wind. Rain began pelting down, making fast-flowing rivers in the gutters. A man in a green uniform appeared at the entrance, peered suspiciously around for a minute or two, then retreated back inside. A bus splashed up the hill and stopped, blocking his view. He stiffened with apprehension until it moved on again. Yet what a depressing view it was, especially through the grey mist of rain. How horrible to have to live in that towering monstrosity, that bleak, soulless giant. He could give Angela such a better place to live. Bearsden was *the* best area. His flat was in the middle of the village, handy for good-quality shops and restaurants. She could have everything she needed there. The best of everything.

Surely she could not have lied to him about loving him and wanting him. She had sounded so desperately sincere. It must be that she was unhappily married and longing to be free so that they could be together. *It must be.*

He seesawed between this certainty and the hopelessness of being able to find her or the husband. Even if he saw her, she might not be with the man.

He clung to the steering wheel, perilously near to tears of frustration and misery. He waited and waited until the early hours when the skyscraper blocks took on a ghostly hue and the park filled with mysterious, rustling shadows.

*****

They started looking at flats together. Just as good mates. That was the idea at first. But to Cheryl's secret delight, they were becoming really close. He had even taken her home to meet his family. His father used to be employed in the Hyde Park Locomotive Works. They built steam engines there, Mr McKechnie boasted, 'exported to more than sixty countries all over the world'.

He liked to reminisce about how everyone used to line the streets to admire the big engines being taken to the Broomielaw and put on to ships for delivery to far-off places like India.

'There's steam locomotives that we built in Springburn still being used abroad. They'll last forever. Marvellous machines.'

There had originally been four great locomotive works in Springburn – Cowlairs, St Rollox, Hyde Park and Atlas, Mr McKechnie said. And at their peak around 1900, they had employed nine thousand men.

'Engines, carriages and wagons were built and repaired for the great British railway companies, especially North British and the Caledonian.'

'For pity's sake, Dad,' Tommy said, 'Cheryl's not interested in all that.'

'Yes, I am,' Cheryl protested. 'Honestly, I think it's fascinating, Mr McKechnie.'

She was a great hit with Mr McKechnie. She wasn't so sure about Mrs McKechnie. But then probably mammies would never believe any girl was good enough for their precious sons. At least Mrs McKechnie was polite enough and treated Cheryl to a nice tea. It was Mrs McKechnie who took an active interest in the flat-hunting.

'I'll keep a look out for anything that's going in Springburn,' she told them. 'A bigger place would be best. That way you could get someone else – maybe another girl – to share and she could help with the rent.'

And stay close to Mammy in Springburn. And maybe prevent me from getting too close to Tommy, Cheryl thought. Maybe Tommy's mum can fool him but she can't fool me. If I can get a place at the opposite end of Glasgow from Springburn, I'll take it.

Tommy was on late shift on the buses and so she went around looking at a few places straight after she finished work in the shopping mall. It wasn't so much fun going on her own. The weather turned rotten as well. Freezing cold and bucketing rain every night, as if winter had come early. She had to wear her beanie hat pulled down over her ears and her jacket hood up for protection. It was just as well Tommy wasn't with her. She felt a right sight and even though she ran as fast as she could, straight from the bus into the shelter of the entrance, she still got soaked. She dripped water on to the brown linoleum tiles and had to give herself a good shake in the lift before emerging out on to the thirtieth floor and going into the house.

'Is that you, hen?' her mother called. 'I've had your tea ready for ages but I've kept it warm in the oven.'

Then when Cheryl entered the living room, 'You'll be getting your death traipsing about in this weather. Where's Tommy?'

'He's on late shift. I told you, Mammy.'

'I don't remember you telling me any such thing. Anyway, fancy him letting you trail about on your own all over the place at night.'

'I was just viewing a few flats. A couple in Pollokshaws and Shawlands and . . .'

'Away over there?' her mother cried out in distress. 'Och Cheryl, I'm sure something nice in Springburn or Balornock would be better. So much handier for your work.'

Cheryl sighed. 'Not you as well.'

'What do you mean?'

'Oh, never mind.'

'You're tired, dear, and no wonder. Sit down here by the fire and I'll bring you a nice bit of fish and a baked potato on a tray.'

'Thanks, Mammy.'

'Did you find any place, by the way?'

'No, not yet.'

Her mother looked relieved. 'Och well, never mind, pet. You've a good home here so there's no hurry.'

'Where's Daddy?' As if she didn't know.

'He's fine. But one of his mates had a wee accident on the line and he's gone to see how he is.'

Cheryl shook her head. Her mother would believe anything. Any time now her father would stagger in acting like a stupid fool, with his singing, his efforts to do some dance steps, his maudlin talk, his slobbering all over both her and her mother.

Cheryl clung to thoughts of being far away with Tommy in a place of their own. She longed for the basic decency, sincerity and comfort of him.

13

'What on earth is she playing at?' Patricia Gordon asked her husband. 'What do you make of this?'

Hamish Gordon accepted the small, gold-edged notelet and stared at it.

'Balgray Hill? That's near Springburn, I think.'

'She has a lovely place in the West End. What on earth is she doing in a slummy place like that?'

'You don't know if it's a slum. It might be all right. I remember reading about all the rebuilding that's going on in that area.'

'But she has such a lovely place in the West End and Eddie works in Byres Road.'

'Why don't you phone her?'

'She doesn't give any phone number. She just says to come and see her at that address on Sunday.'

'And she'll explain, she says, so just try and be patient.'

'Her job was in the West End. Such a nice private nursery school. Surely she can't have left that good nursery school?'

'Just try and be patient for another day,' Hamish repeated. 'I'll drive you through to Glasgow on Sunday.'

'Maybe I should phone Eddie.'

'No, I don't think so, Pat.'

'Why not? I'm terribly worried.'

'It may be a bit of trouble between them and she wouldn't want you to interfere.'

'What trouble? They were perfectly happy together the last I heard. And it's not so long ago we visited them, remember? They were perfectly happy then. She can't have just up and left him.' Patricia shook her head. 'Anyway, it's not like Sandra. She wouldn't have the nerve.'

'We'll find out exactly what's happened on Sunday.'

'I just hope she's done nothing silly that she'll live to regret. She's always been a bit naive and easily influenced. I hope to goodness there isn't some awful man who has . . .'

'Patricia!' Hamish groaned. 'You're letting that over-active imagination of yours run away with you. I thought you said you had some shopping to do.'

'Oh, all right.'

She went for her tweed jacket, then collected her leather purse and her green shopping bag with the thistle decoration. After popping an umbrella into the bag 'just in case', she kissed the top of her husband's head.

'I won't be long, dear.'

He had already picked up and opened his *Scotsman* newspaper.

'Fine.'

She left the downstairs flat and made her way along the High Street. It was a cosy little flat with an ever-changing view, especially in the tourist season. That was all very well but she and Hamish had been looking for a bigger place in the New Town. Admittedly, she enjoyed sitting at her window or strolling along the street watching all the foreigners with their expensive cameras taking pictures of places like John Knox's house with its top-storey wooden gallery and the City Chambers and Brodie's Court. Brodie's Court was the home of Edinburgh's most colourful citizen, Deacon Brodie, a respectable cabinetmaker and town councillor by day and a burglar by night. He had been hanged eventually on a gallows of his own design. He had bribed the hangman to allow him to wear a steel collar so that he could survive the rope but his gallows proved too efficient.

The old town had a fascinating history and was endlessly interesting but the New Town was elegant and beautiful and Patricia had always wanted to live there.

Sandra used to have that ambition too. But of course she'd fallen in love with Eddie and he was a Glasgow man. According to Sandra, it was a fairytale romance and, almost straight from college, she'd married Eddie, got a job in Glasgow and, as far as Sandra had led her to believe, lived happily ever after.

What on earth had gone wrong? Patricia had to post some airmail letters in the post office and while she was there, the temptation to phone Eddie overcame her.

She went into one of the booths and dialled the number.

'Hello?'

His voice sounded strange, different.

Oh dear, she thought. He's upset and unhappy.

'It's me, Eddie. Patricia. I was wondering what has happened. I got a letter from Sandra this morning – just a few lines really, telling me to visit her on the Balgray Hill on Sunday – a place called The Heights. What on earth is she doing there?'

There was a long silence.

'Eddie? Are you still there? Are you all right?'

'Yes, I'm all right.'

'What's happened?'

'Sandra walked out on me.'

'Oh dear. I am sorry to hear that. I thought you were so happy together.'

'I thought so too.'

'Is there anything I can do? Do you want me to try and speak to her or what?'

'No but thanks all the same. I'll have to go now, Patricia. Thanks for phoning.'

The line went dead.

★★★★★

It was their Friday get-together and Alice, Rita, Sandra, wee Mary and Janet and two past residents had gathered with Betty and Dorothy in the meeting room. The two past residents had been getting on great in their new homes.

'I've never been so happy,' one of them called Eve said and her friend, Flora, agreed.

'It's been a completely new start, a whole new life.'

'Any new men?' Betty asked.

'No way!' Eve's voice loudened, her eyes bulged. 'I'll never trust another man – never again!'

'Bastards,' Betty agreed, with a toss of her hair. Then a hint of laughter glimmered in her eyes. 'Sometimes I still lust after them, though.'

Dorothy came through with the trolley and began passing the teacups round. The children, who had been playing in the opposite corner, skipped across the room to make sure of a share of the iced sponge cake.

'I know how Eve feels.' Dorothy cut the cake and handed a plate to each of the women and to the two children. Her hair had been dyed blonde but her roots were needing done. 'It took me ages to get over my marriage and I still don't feel able to tackle another man.'

'Tackle?' Betty laughed. 'Sounds like a rugby match.'

Dorothy flashed a dimpled grin. 'You know what I mean.'

Flora enjoyed a mouthful of cake. 'I wouldn't mind. They can't all be the same. There's bound to be some nice men around.' She giggled. 'There's a tall, dark and handsome guy started work in my office. I really fancy him. Do none of you miss sex? I mean apart from Betty.'

'I never get the time these days.' Dorothy helped herself to a piece of cake.

'Me neither,' Betty said. 'I feel really deprived. I'm thinking of buying one of those sex toys, or whatever you call them.'

They all laughed then.

'At least it'll no' batter you, hen,' wee Mary said. 'Let us know if it works and we'll all put an order in.'

The children had wandered over to the window while still enjoying their cake. Suddenly Bobby cried out, 'Mummy, I think there's a man with a gun down there!'

'What?'

They all nearly knocked the tea trolley over in their rush. There, far below, like a mechanical toy, was the figure of a man waving his hand about. It did indeed look as if he was clutching a gun.

'Oh my God, oh my God!' Sandra began shaking so much she could no longer stand up. Betty had to catch her and hold her. 'Oh my God, it's Eddie.'

Just then, the office phone rang. Dorothy ran to answer it. In a couple of minutes, she had returned.

'It's the concierge. He's dialled 999. It's Sandra's husband, right enough. He's been shouting for Sandra. But he won't know what floor we're on and Monty's managed to lock the entrance door.

Sandra was gasping and sobbing.

'I knew he was going to kill me. I knew it.'

Rita was wild-eyed and clutched Bobby and Susie against her. 'He's obviously a madman. He's going to kill the lot of us.'

'Oh my God!' Sandra's voice flew high in hysteria. 'Oh my God!'

Taken aback, the children began to wail. Betty put her hand over Sandra's mouth.

'You're frightening the children.'

Wee Mary said, 'See bloody men!'

14

Monty could see the increasingly agitated figure outside. He'd managed to lock the door by pressing the emergency button at his desk and had phoned 999. As soon as he'd said the man had a gun, he had got instant action. He was told an armed response team was on its way. His brother-in-law was a police officer and had once told him something that few ordinary Glasgow folk knew. There was always an armed response team cruising around Glasgow twenty-four hours a day. Monty could only hope that it was in the Springburn area at the moment and not over in Govan or elsewhere.

Meantime he prayed the door would hold. He also frantically dialled everybody's number and told them to get out of their flats and on to the fire escape stairway. Outside, the man had gone totally berserk and was throwing himself at the door. It was shuddering and groaning ominously with each assault. Monty could feel the cold sweat of fear trickling down his chest, his shirt sticking to his chest. 'Sweet Jesus, let the bloody door hold!'

There was a momentary pause outside as the maniacal figure stopped to regain his breath and rethink his strategy.

He tried lifting his foot high and stomping it out, smashing against the lock.

The door still held.

Where were the bloody polis? It seemed an age since he'd called them. Monty clung on to the edge of his desk, knuckles white with tension.

Outside, the man stepped back and, with his left hand, covered his face with his jacket collar. He pointed the gun towards the door and, shutting his eyes, pulled the trigger. There was an almighty bang as the shot was fired; his first effort hit the door frame. This time aiming properly, he fired again and the entire reinforced glass door disintegrated before him. Arms crossed over his face, he burst into the foyer.

'For God's sake, son, screw the nut. Ye'll get yersel' killed.' Monty desperately tried to get him to listen but the man was incensed.

'Where's that bitch? Where's my fucking wife?'

Still gamely trying to calm things down, Monty continued to talk in a quiet, soothing voice. 'It's no' worth it. Think this through.'

They both were talking simultaneously, Monty quietly and the intruder shouting and waving his gun.

Eventually the man lost patience and, leaping over the desk, grabbed Monty by his shirt front. He jabbed the barrel of the gun hard into Monty's temple repeatedly, emphasising his words, 'Tell me where she is or your head will be sprayed all over that fucking wall.'

Monty could hold out no longer. Now really in fear of his life, he pointed to the lift. 'The tenth floor, that's where the refuge is.' His final act of defiance was to direct the madman to the wrong floor. Hopefully that would at least give the armed police time to arrive and the residents time to escape down the stairs.

Then no sooner had the lift creaked closed, than there was the screeching of tyres braking under stress. Monty looked through the shattered door to see police cars and vans outside, vomiting out sinister black-clad policemen, armed to the teeth and wearing armoured Kevlar chest protectors.

Monty shouted, 'He's on the lift going to the tenth floor. He's mad and he's gonnae kill somebody for sure.'

Some policemen stayed in the foyer covering the lift doors and directing residents who were nervously emerging from the stairs to gather outside on the street. The rest of the police crashed through the fire doors out on to the stairwell. 'Go, go, go!' They thundered up the stairs, hearts pounding from both exertion and adrenalin.

Cursing inside the lift, the gunman impatiently thumped his fist into the wall. What was wrong with this piece of shit of a lift? It seemed to creep upwards.

Finally, after what seemed an age, it arrived at floor ten. He burst out on to the landing, red eyes staring, waving his gun around in front of him. He grabbed the first door handle he saw and thrust his shoulder forward. Locked. This time he brooked no delay and blasted the lock to smithereens.

The armed response team heard the shot. They redoubled their efforts and pounded upwards.

The door swung back crazily on its hinges as the gunman burst into the flat. An empty flat. Cursing, he went back out on to the landing. He tried the next door. He listened intently. He thought he could hear whimpering inside.

Stepping back from the door, he fired once more, smashing the lock. Then suddenly the fire escape door burst open.

'Drop the gun!'

The gunman swung round on them, gun raised. Three shots immediately hit him square in the chest, knocking him back. Slowly, eyes vacant now, he slid down the wall to sit slumped at its foot. A large red streak smeared the wall behind him.

Not just Sandra but all the women in the refuge were in a state of collapse. Even Betty and Dorothy were visibly shaken. They tried their best, however, to calm all the women down as well as comfort Sandra.

'It's all over,' they kept repeating. 'We're safe now.'

Sandra was sobbing uncontrollably.

'He was my husband.'

Wee Mary suddenly burst out, 'So what? For God's sake, Sandra, ye're well rid of him. Think yersel' lucky he's gone.'

Betty had phoned for the doctor and she kept striding impatiently over to the window hoping for a sight of his car.

At last she was able to call out, 'Here's the doctor. He'll soon make you all feel better.'

She hastened from the room to open the door and wait for the doctor emerging from the lift. By the time he had entered the room, Sandra had collapsed back in her chair, eyes closed, breathless, moaning sounds issuing from tightly closed lips.

All the others were white-faced and wide-eyed.

As the doctor attended to Sandra, his soothing voice and presence had a calming effect on everyone, even before he gave them prescriptions for medication.

After he'd gone Betty said again, 'It's all over. We're safe now.'

And they all tried to believe her.

15

The last thing on earth John Ingram expected, as he sat in the car watching for Angela and her husband, was a mad gunman. At first he was paralysed with shock and fear. He just sat hunched forward, unconscious of a lock of black hair covering one side of his face, long fingers glued round the steering wheel, eyes bulging. The man was bawling and waving a gun about. In his shocked state, Ingram thought the man was bawling out Angela's name. He couldn't move. Then he heard the first shot and panicked. The car stalled. It seemed an eternity before he managed to get it going. He had no recollection of how he drove through the busy streets and eventually arrived in Bearsden.

Automatically he parked the car in the car park behind the shops. He half-ran to his close. Up the stairs, two at a time, into his flat and then he collapsed on to a chair, heart leaping up to his throat. After a time, he was able to pour a double whisky and knock it back. He managed to light a cigarette. Gradually he calmed down.

It took him the best part of a week, however, to return to normal. He worked every day in the shop. He chatted to the other barbers and to the customers as if nothing unusual had happened. But he couldn't get the incident out of his mind.

He read about it in the paper and watched a report about it on STV and discovered it wasn't Angela but a woman called Sandra the man was after. His relief was overwhelming.

The occupants of the high-rise flats – or most of them – had been evacuated. Now *there* would have been a good chance to see Angela and maybe the husband too, as they all streamed out of the building. If only he had waited and kept watching. Apparently there was a women's refuge somewhere in the building and this Sandra person was hiding in it. The gunman had tracked her down.

Probably he's suffered the same or similar cruel treatment from his Sandra, as I have suffered from my Angela, Ingram thought.

The poor guy had been caught, killed in a shootout with the police. He must have been mad, thinking he could get away with brandishing a gun for all to see and bringing everyone's attention to him by bawling abuse in a public place. He was just asking to be caught.

'But I'm not mad,' Ingram thought. 'I'll quietly wait and watch and, once I find Angela's husband, I'll follow him away from the building. I'll take my time. I'll follow him to his work. Any place away from the Balgray Hill. I'll get him on his own. No one will ever know. An open razor is so efficient. And quiet.'

It was another week before he saw Angela and her husband. He could hardly contain his excitement when he spotted the lovely blonde-haired girl in the white trouser suit emerge. Then rage rushed in like a red-hot flood burning away every other emotion. She was hanging on to the man's arm, gazing lovingly up at him.

'How could she have lied to me so convincingly?' Ingram asked himself incredulously. Night after night, her voice had caressed him. Her words had been not only loving but passionate. She swore she loved him and him alone. Obviously she was just making a fool of him. Listening to him, not with the loving, caring sympathy she had led him to believe but with secret yawns and probably even laughter. Probably her husband had been there. His head throbbed to bursting point with fury at the thought.

The man wasn't even good-looking. A stocky-built guy with red hair. He was dressed in a cheap T-shirt and denims with ragged holes and frayed edges. The couple walked along past his car. The man was so close he could read the words on his T-shirt – 'I still hate Maggie Thatcher'.

A bloody Communist to boot!

He watched them stroll into the park. He got out of the car and followed them. He fingered the razor in his pocket. He waited for his chance. But it was Sunday and the park was full of strolling lovers and children kicking balls and old people sitting on benches. He had to give up eventually. People were beginning to stare at him. Or so he imagined.

At least now he knew what they both looked like. There would be other, better opportunities. He wasn't the fool Angela obviously took him for. He wasn't going to get caught.

He still could hardly credit it when he phoned at his usual six o'clock and she answered him as if nothing had happened. Her voice, as usual, was so loving, so soft, so gentle. He had once asked her if she came from the Highlands because of the lovely lilt in her voice. It had none of the broad Glasgow accents. She said both her parents originally came from up north.

'Are you all right, John?' she asked. 'You're very quiet this evening. I hope you're not still upset about us not meeting. I can't explain, John. But believe me, it would be a terrible disappointment to you if we ever did meet.'

Why would that be then? he thought derisively. Because you'd bring your husband along?

'You're probably right,' he managed. 'I won't mention it again.'

But we will meet, he determined, and I will more than just mention it. I'll tell you what a lying, two-faced, money-grubbing bitch you really are. At the same time, he wished it could have been different. He longed to the point of tears for it to be different. Now he knew that in appearance at least, she was even more beautiful and desirable than he had imagined.

Again he went back to working normally in the shop. His work was proving something of a therapy. It helped to distract him and calm him down. After a few days he felt enough in control of his thoughts and emotions to return to Balgrayhill Road. This time he had no luck. There was no sign of Angela or the red-haired man. He arrived on the hill day after day and returned home night after night, still without a glimpse of either of them.

Then one day he had to take a bus into town to an alteration tailor to have a suit taken in. He was thin at the best of times but recently he'd lost weight and his clothes were now hanging too loosely on his tall skeletal frame. He could hardly believe his eyes. There, sitting in the driver's seat of the bus, was the red-haired man.

16

The trouble was, wee Mary *had* gone back on the 'hard stuff'. Janet, Alice, Sandra and Rita had a secret conference about it while Mary was out at the shops one day. She kept all right during the day when Betty and Dorothy were on duty. Once the girls went off duty in the evening, however, it was clear to see that Mary got steadily drunk. On several occasions now, she'd drunk herself into oblivion and Janet, with the help of Sandra, had to put the unconscious Mary to bed.

Opinion was divided on what should be done. Should they report wee Mary to Betty? Or should they wait in the hope that once Mary got over the trauma of the gunman incident, she would return to normal and need nothing more than her daily teapot of beer?

As if the one dreadful trauma was not enough, they all had to suffer another. It brought the problem with Mary to a climax.

Janet had, for the first time, gone into town for the evening. It had given her great pleasure to dress in her designer label outfit and Hermes scarf. There had been a concert in the Royal Concert Hall and she had persuaded Sandra to attend it with her. Sandra's nerves had been in a terrible state and the doctor had to give her a sedative. However, she shared Janet's love of classical music and it was an evening of Mozart that they gone to. They had invited Mary to come with them but she had laughed.

'Och, you know fine it's no' ma thing. I couldn't even spell the man's name. But thanks for askin'. Away ye go, the pair of ye, an' enjoy yersels.'

So they had gone. And it had done Sandra good. They had both thoroughly enjoyed the evening. They'd treated themselves to a taxi home. They'd had to share the lift with the awful man from the thirtieth floor who was a terrible drunk and who sang at the pitch of this voice and tried to dance with Sandra. But up to that point, it was the only incident that had spoiled the lovely evening.

They smelled burning the moment they unlocked the flat door. They both ran along the lobby and into the living room. At the first sight of Mary, Sandra immediately fainted. Somehow Janet managed to pull the unconscious body of Mary away from the electric fire. Her arm had burned through the flesh to the bone. Once she'd separated Mary from the fire, Janet ran to the phone and dialled for an ambulance. Then she dragged Sandra away from the living room in case she came to and saw the extent of Mary's horrific injuries. As soon as Sandra did come to, Janet helped her into the kitchen, sat her on a stool and gave her a drink of water. She gulped at some water herself.

'I've just sent for an ambulance. We'll have to wait until it comes. I'm frightened to touch Mary in case I make things worse. We'll have to wait for the ambulance,' she repeated. 'She must have got drunk and fallen unconscious on to the fire.'

'We shouldn't have left her,' Sandra moaned.

'Mary wouldn't want us to be prisoners in the house because of her. Anyway, this was the first night out we've had and we asked her to come with us.'

'Oh my God,' Sandra caught her fingers in her curls. 'That *smell*. It's burning flesh. It's . . .'

'Be quiet, Sandra.' Janet's voice was unusually sharp and authoritative. 'Pull yourself together. You're not doing yourself or anybody any good acting like a drama queen.'

Within minutes, they could hear the faint wail of the ambulance approaching in the street below. Janet went to open the door in readiness for the ambulance men emerging from the lift.

'It's Mary McFee,' she told them immediately they appeared. 'Through in the living room. She fell against the fire. It's her arm. She's unconscious.'

The men strode past her and along the lobby. Janet didn't follow them. She couldn't face seeing Mary's injuries again. She could only pray that she was still alive. The ambulance men reappeared with the still-unconscious woman on a stretcher.

'Where are you taking her?' she asked.

'The Royal,' one of the men said. 'Best to phone in the morning and see how she is. There's no point in an elderly lady like yourself coming out at this time of night to hang about – probably for hours – in a hospital waiting room. Phone and see how she is in the morning and when she'll be allowed any visitors.'

Reluctantly, Janet closed the door after them and returned to the kitchen.

'They're taking her to the Royal,' she told an ashen-faced Sandra. 'We'll find out how she is tomorrow.'

'I feel sick.'

'Be sick then. I'm going to open all the windows, then put the kettle on.'

Sandra began retching over the sink. Janet opened the kitchen window, then hurried away to open the rest in an effort to get rid of the smell. She felt far from well herself. Averting her eyes from the electric fire, she switched it off.

Poor Mary, she kept thinking. Poor wee Mary. She'd really ruined everything for herself now. Drink was not allowed in the refuge. It was a strict rule. There would be no hiding the fact that she was drunk and a danger to herself and others. She stank of whisky. She must have spent most of her benefit money on it.

But at least, Janet prayed, let her survive this. Please don't let her die.

Both she and Sandra asked Alice for one of her sleeping tablets but it was quite a time before they were able to return to their flat and collapse into bed. Alice and Rita insisted on being told everything and it was shock, horror all over again.

Next morning, even before Betty and Dorothy came on duty, Janet phoned the hospital. Mary had survived but she'd had her arm amputated. Janet felt unwell again. She had to go and sit down and leave Sandra to tell Betty and Dorothy.

The girls came in immediately and Betty said, 'Poor wee Mary. You did well, Janet. Sandra tells me you calmly took charge of the situation, helped Mary, helped Sandra, sent for the ambulance and so on.'

'I don't know about calmly,' Janet said.

Betty glanced at her watch. 'I'll go and visit her right away. I shouldn't be too long. I'll come in as soon as I get back and let you know exactly how she is.'

'I'm going to go too,' Janet said.

'No, no, Janet. You don't look fit enough to go anywhere. Not today. Leave it to me just now.'

Janet was secretly relieved. She felt quite faint. After Betty left to go and visit the hospital, Sandra rallied to her aid.

'You relax through in the living room and watch television or read the paper, I'll make us a cup of coffee and then I'll see to the lunch.'

'Thank you, Sandra. I'm feeling my age today, I think. I haven't an ounce of energy left.'

'I don't think sleeping tablets give you a refreshing sleep, do you? I mean, they can knock you out but next day you don't feel much benefit.'

'Yes, you're right. I'm not going to take one tonight.'

'How about if I go down to Springburn and get some herbal tablets? I sometimes used to take valerian and lemon balm. You can get lemon balm tea as well. Or lemon balm and valerian tea. It's very soothing, I always found.'

'That sounds just what we need, dear. Yes, I'd appreciate that.'

'I'll wait until Betty comes back and then I'll go.'

'That's kind of you, Sandra. I appreciate it.'

'The fresh air will do me good and getting out of the house for a wee while as well. I mean, every time I look at that fire, I . . .'

'Yes, all right, Sandra. That's the kettle boiling. If you make the coffee, I'll just go through and have a few minutes' rest.'

Actually she would have preferred to go to bed but she resisted the temptation. Betty had said she was strong and she *was* strong. She would get over this, as she had got over everything else. It was true what Betty said. Well, she never actually said the words, 'You are no longer the stuttering, fearful, nervous wreck that you once were.' But Janet knew that's what she meant. That pathetic woman had gone. She was strong now. With great determination, she kept repeating the words to herself.

After an hour or two resting quietly against the deep green cushions of the chair with the fresh air from the window wafting in, she began to feel better. Sounds from far down on the road filtered faintly in with the breeze, not upsetting her with their coarse laughter and broad Glasgow accents as they once had. Now they had the familiarity of home. She dozed off for a time. She was awakened by Sandra setting the table for lunch.

'Sit where you are, Janet. I'll give you it over on a tray.'

'No, no, I'm fine now, thanks. I'd rather come to the table.'

'Betty was in earlier but we thought it best not to waken you. We thought the rest would do you good.'

'Yes, I do feel much better. But what about Mary?'

'She's still poorly after the operation. But she's going to be all right.'

'Thank goodness.'

'What does Betty think? Does she know the truth about what happened?'

'They told her at the hospital. I bet Mary's blood was full of alcohol. Betty didn't say exactly but she questioned me about the whisky. She saw the bottle in the kitchen, of course. I told her quite truthfully that we hadn't seen her bringing *whisky* in.' Sandra's eyes widened. 'I mean we didn't, did we?'

'Maybe we should have told her about the beer.'

'Mary was all right with the beer.'

'Yes, she was, right enough,' Janet agreed.

'It must have been that madman I was married to that caused her to take something stronger,' Sandra said. 'She'd probably thought it would help to calm her. She tried to act brave, like she always does, but she was really devastated.'

'We all were, Sandra, but poor Mary always had her drink problem.'

'Fancy her losing an arm. That's terrible. I feel it's really my fault.'

'How on earth . . . ?'

'Well, he was my husband and, if I hadn't been here and if I hadn't . . .'

'Oh, you do go on,' Janet interrupted impatiently. 'What we'll have to think about now is how we can help Mary.'

Sandra nodded.

'I do, don't I? I've never had much confidence in myself.

'Sandra!' Janet groaned.

'Oh, sorry.'

'Mary will have a lot of readjusting to do. Coping with only one arm.'

'I hope they don't put her out. I'll feel terrible about that.'

'Surely they won't. It would be too cruel. How would she manage? Where could she go? No, I can't imagine Betty doing that.'

'They won't at first anyway because Betty said they told her that once Mary's home, a nurse will come regularly to dress . . .' Sandra shuddered 'the stump.'

'I can't imagine her drinking again. Not after this, surely. But we must try to get her to go out more. Not just to the shops and back. We should take her into town to the cinema perhaps. And for walks in the park. Anything to give her an interest and keep her off drink.'

'Yes, we should all get out more. I was just saying that to Alice the other day. She's worse than ever, by the way. She's frightened to put a foot over the door. Rita said an old neighbour had seen her in the park and she's terrified he'll tell her husband where she is.'

'Did he actually see her come in here?'

'No. Rita says she's sure there's no need for her to feel so scared. Alice agrees but still refuses to go out. She just can't, she says.'

'She'll get over it in time,' Janet said. 'Especially once she gets another house.'

'Rita says Alice wants to move to another town. Betty's going to see what can be done about that. But first they've to go and see a lawyer about Alice's divorce. I know how she feels. I was terrified to put a foot over the door. I know this will sound awful but I used to secretly wish my husband was dead. Now he is, maybe I wished it on him.'

'Nonsense but I know how you feel,' Janet said. And she did. Exactly.

17

Each multi-storey building, Mabel thought, was like a separate village. She knew nothing of the people or what went on in the other tower blocks, like Viewpoint, but, in The Heights, she was aware of all the gossip. She overheard things in the lift, or echoing on the landings, or while she was disposing of her rubbish. Nothing really newsworthy had ever happened in all the years she'd been living in the flat. Until recently. Of course crime, especially drug-related crime, was on the increase all over the country, indeed the world. Or so she had read in the newspapers and learned from the television. But gun crime? She'd never heard about such a thing in Glasgow. Who would have thought of anything so violent happening right on her own doorstep, so to speak?

Razors, yes. She's heard of razor gangs. But not nowadays and not here. She'd once read a book about razor-wielding gangs in the Gorbals. But that was a novel. The author had probably made it all up. She'd certainly never seen or heard of any such things in Springburn or Balornock. There was drunkenness. And she suspected there might be drug-taking going on among the crowds of youths that often hung about outside the building. But nothing, as far as she knew, really serious. Or at least, nothing considered newsworthy. Until the photographs of The Heights, outside and inside, were splashed all over the papers.

It made her think about moving. She had a few fond memories of her schooldays in the Highlands, walking though the beautiful countryside, along peaceful country roads, seeing people in cottages hanging up washing. People's friendly greetings in passing. But those were far-off days. Her parents had moved to Glasgow when she was still quite young, first to the old tenements and then to this high-rise flat. She knew no one in the Highlands now. She would be as lonely there as she was here. Anyway, she didn't feel fit enough now to cope with all the upheaval of moving house.

Indeed, she felt it quite an ordeal to cope even with living here. Her arthritis wasn't getting any better. The doctor said it was 'just wear and tear'. *Just!* Had he no idea of the pain and disability involved? At one time she had treated herself to little outings across in the park, especially if there was a concert or some other event going on. Sometimes she'd even take a packed lunch and sit on one of the park seats and watch whatever was happening. Maybe she should start doing that again. There used to be a brass band playing. It might have been the Salvation Army – she couldn't remember – but she had enjoyed it. She wasn't so keen on the Orange Walk parade which sometimes ended up in the park. She remembered how they used to purposely march past any local Catholic church and bang their drums as loud as they could as they did so. It had made her feel nervous. They always seemed too provocative, always looking for a fight.

Nowadays, it was becoming a struggle to venture any further than the park. To go into town to Marks & Spencer's for food, for instance, was becoming more of an ordeal than a pleasure. What would happen if she became completely housebound? She had no daughter, no 'good girl', to slave after her. Not that she would have made a slave of a daughter if she'd been lucky enough to have one. She still felt some bitterness towards her mother and father. Especially her mother.

However, what was the use of feeling like that now? The past was past. She had to concentrate on making the best she could of the present and just pray that the future wouldn't be as bad as she feared. What she feared as much as anything, of course, was being without John. He hadn't phoned for a few nights and she thought that was an end of it. But now, he had phoned again explaining that he had been away from home on business. He said how good it was to hear her lovely Highland voice again.

She had laughed. 'I've lived in Glasgow for years, John. I consider myself a Glaswegian now.'

'I bet your parents never lost their Highland accent.'

'Well, no. But they had lived there much longer than I had.'

'You haven't lost it either. And I'm glad. It makes you different from anyone else I've ever known. It makes you special.'

Later in the conversation, he'd said, 'Did you read in the paper about the gun siege?'

She immediately became wary. 'Yes.'

'Terrible, wasn't it?'

'Yes. You don't expect guns in Glasgow. That's the sort of thing that happens more in America, isn't it?'

'It wasn't near where you live, then?'

She felt a flurry of distress. 'No, of course not. What makes you say that?'

'I care about you, darling. I don't want you to be in any danger.'

'Well, anyway, it's all over now. The gunman's dead. He must have been mad to go berserk like that. And with a gun!'

'Yes. If he'd wanted to kill somebody that badly, there are quieter ways of doing it.'

'You're giving me the shivers, John. For goodness' sake, let's talk about something else.'

'Sorry. It was just something everybody's been talking about.'

'I know but . . .'

'I am sorry if I've upset you, Angela. I won't say another word about it. What have you been doing since I've been away?'

'Oh, just working and coming home and watching television or reading.'

'Where did you say you worked?'

'I didn't.' She was beginning to feel very uneasy. 'We agreed, John. We were never going to know each other's true identity. Never going to meet.'

'No, it was you who said . . .'

'Yes, you did, right from the beginning, John. It's the rule with these calls and you've always known that. I'm so sorry that your feelings have changed like this. Everything was so perfect before.'

'Perfect?' His voice was incredulous. 'How can any relationship be perfect that's just voices over a phone?'

'I'm so sorry. I really thought you were as content and as happy as I was.'

'Content?' He gave a bitter laugh. It didn't sound like her John at all.

'Is there somebody else, Angela? Please tell me the truth. I think I at least deserve the truth.'

She hesitated. Yes, he did deserve the truth but the words – I'm old enough to be your mother or even your grandmother. I'm old and I'm ugly – refused to be spoken out loud. She couldn't bear to say them. They were too cruel.

'I don't love anybody else,' she managed. 'I never have and that's the truth.'

'Well then . . .'

'Please, John, please don't keep going on about this. There's a perfectly good reason for us not meeting, believe me.'

'You love me.' He seemed to be talking to himself. 'And I love you.'

'John, I'm sorry. I'll have to go now.'

She hastily replaced the receiver. Then caught up in a wild hurricane of grief, she wept uncontrollably. Oh, what she would give to be young and beautiful. She would have sold her soul to the devil to be young and beautiful right now.

18

Cheryl felt depressed. She missed Tommy. He had taken a virus that had been so severe he had to go home early from work. He couldn't even talk over the phone. He had been retching and vomiting so much. His mother had told her, 'Best not to phone again for a few days.'

'Can I come and see him, then?'

'No, definitely not. He's retching his heart up. I'm running back and forward with a basin all the time. He wouldn't want you to see him like that. The doctor says it's an airborne virus that's going around and a lot of people have contracted it. Tommy will phone you when he's well enough.'

She had to be content with that. But she missed him. She missed their chats over the phone. She missed their walks through the park. She missed their journeys around different districts looking for a flat to rent. Some of the prices were outrageous. They'd always gone for a coffee or a drink afterwards and sat discussing whatever flat it was they'd seen.

She began to worry. It upset her to think of Tommy being distressed and ill. She wanted to be with him to help him. They'd had a photo taken together and she kept taking it out and looking at it. Sometimes, when no one was looking, she kissed it. She even began to worry in case Mrs McKechnie was lying and in some devious way trying to keep her and Tommy apart. Days at work floated by like a dream.

Then the world changed. Tommy didn't just phone. He arrived at The Heights. Monty let him in downstairs. Her mother answered the doorbell and then called out in a wavering voice, 'Cheryl, it's Tommy to see you.'

Forgetting to put on her usual casual act in front of her mother and father, she rushed from her bedroom into the lobby and flung her arms around Tommy's neck.

'I've been so worried about you.'

Her mother gave a trembling smile and retreated into the living room. From there, her father's drunken voice roared out, 'That you, Tommy? C'mon in, son. C'mon in an' have a wee refreshment.'

'Let's go for a walk across in the park,' she suggested in desperation.

Tommy grinned and nodded. Then as soon as they'd left the house, his arms tightened around her and he kissed her passionately on the mouth. The kiss would have lasted longer but it was interrupted by some neighbours spilling out of the lift.

Tommy quickly dragged Cheryl into the lift before the door closed and they went plummeting down. Another kiss was spoiled by the door opening at the twenty-third floor and Betty, the refuge worker, like a mother hen led in two worried-looking women from the refuge. Betty smiled at them. She had such a calm, sympathetic, yet strong face. There were times when Cheryl wished she lived in the refuge and could depend on Betty to sort out her troubles.

'How's wee Mary?' she asked. 'I was that sorry to hear about her accident.'

'We're on our way to see her now. We'll let you know . . .'

'We found her, Janet and me,' a saucer-eyed Sandra interrupted. 'It was absolutely horrific.'

'Here we are,' Betty said cheerfully as the lift jerked to a halt. 'I'll tell Mary you were asking for her. Bye.'

Cheryl returned Betty's wave and felt amused at the way the big refuge worker was herding the women away along the road.

Tommy's arm was around her waist and more than anything, Cheryl felt happy. There was no doubt now in her mind that she loved him. Now if they found a flat together, she wanted to share not just his bed but his life. As they strolled through the park, arms around each other's waist, they didn't talk at first. They were both so content and so happy. Eventually Cheryl managed, 'Are you all right now, Tommy? I really was worried about you. I've heard of people dying of these bugs.'

'I'm fine. It'll take more than a wee bug to finish me off. I'll tell you one thing, though. I was dying to tell you I saw an advert in a local shop about a flat in Kay Street. It's just minutes away from your work. I know you're a bit fed up working in the shopping centre but with the sports centre just across the road from the flat, with the gym and the pool and the library and God knows what all else in one building, you could try for a job there.'

'Oh, that's wonderful, Tommy. When'll we go and see it? Could we go now, right away? I can't wait.'

Tommy laughed.

'We've an appointment to view tomorrow night. It's the earliest I could get. The factor said the folk in it aren't moving out until tomorrow afternoon. He's doing us a favour because of it being a Saturday. His office is shut then but he says the folks moving out will leave the key with the man next door.'

Cheryl did a skip of delight.

'I'm so excited. I'll not be able to sleep a wink tonight. I'm not usually able to sleep on a Friday because of my dad bawling and singing and it makes me so mad. But tonight I won't care. I'll just be so happy looking forward to tomorrow night.'

She gazed adoringly up at his freckled face and thick mop of red hair. 'Are you happy about it as well, Tommy? I mean, about us moving in together?'

He answered her with a gentle kiss and a murmur of, 'I can't wait.'

She could see the love in his eyes and she clung to him in gratitude.

Never, in any of her romantic, escapist dreams and imaginings, had she ever felt like this – totally happy and safe. It was at that moment she felt Tommy stiffen. He turned away from her and called out angrily to someone nearby, 'What the hell do you think you're staring at?'

Cheryl followed his stare. A man was standing nearby. He had obviously been spying on them. She didn't like the look of him. He was exceptionally tall, with hunched shoulders and bulging eyes and Adam's apple. Some sort of weirdo or pervert, he looked. As if reading her thoughts, Tommy called out, 'Some sort of pervert, are you?'

The man had a hand in one of his pockets and as he moved towards them, a frightening thought suddenly occurred to Cheryl. Maybe this was another mad gunman. Jut then the quiet darkness of the park was shattered by a crowd of young men guffawing and girls screeching with laughter. They looked drunk, staggering and pushing each other about.

'Let's get out of here,' Cheryl pleaded. 'We're not going to get any peace.'

The man disappeared. At least, she was thankful for that.

'We could walk further along among the trees,' Tommy said.

'No, if you don't mind, Tommy, I'm still a bit unnerved with that gun carry-on. I haven't managed to get completely over it yet. I thought I had but I haven't. None of us has. It was such an awful frightening thing to happen.'

'Aye, OK,' Tommy said. 'I'll meet you tomorrow at your work. I've to catch the neighbour before he goes out so I'll call for the key first.'

'I'm sorry to be acting so daft.'

'You're not acting daft at all. It's perfectly understandable. It'll take a while for everybody in The Heights to get over what happened. But don't worry. We'll have plenty of time to be alone together after tomorrow. I know these flats and I'm sure it'll suit us fine. It's only a one room and kitchen, though. It's OK for me but will a wee place like that be OK for you?'

'Great, great.' Cheryl hugged his arm in reassurance. 'Oh, Tommy, we're going to be so happy.'

Her voice was like a hallelujah.

19

Rita Jamieson tried not to look worried or nervous as she waved goodbye to the children. Dorothy was taking them and some children from a couple of other refuges to the seaside for the day. Bobby and Susie had become fond of Dorothy and Rita trusted her. Both Betty and Dorothy were their guardian angels. Every day she thanked God for them and for the refuge. But her secret terror remained. It might not have been so bad if her husband had lived and worked in one town – any town. Then she would know where he was and perhaps that would have helped. The fact that he was a commercial traveller and she never knew where he might be increased her fear a thousandfold.

He might be at Largs today and see the children. If he did, he would snatch them up and, with the best will in the world, Dorothy wouldn't be able to do anything about it. He was a big, powerful man and he was the children's father.

And, as one of her neighbours had once laughingly remarked, 'Your husband could charm the birds off the trees. No wonder he's so successful at his job.'

Not that his charm would fool Dorothy. But if necessary, he could and would take them from her by force.

Dorothy had said, however, that it wasn't fair to the children to keep them tied to their mother's apron strings all the time. They needed to live as normal a life as possible and a day at the seaside would do them so much good. They would have great fun, especially with a crowd of other children to play with.

And so, as cheerfully as possible, she'd waved goodbye to the children. She stood in front of the building for a few more minutes watching Dorothy's people carrier disappear into the distance. Then fear, like a fountain of water, iced up her spine. It was as if her husband was creeping up behind her. She hurried through the entrance and into the lift, not even acknowledging the concierge's greeting. Monty was always ready and willing to have a chat but she couldn't get back quickly enough to the safety of the refuge.

For a short time, she'd thought she was beginning to conquer her fear. She'd even taken the children over to the park a few times. Then there had been the dreadful gun incident and photographs of The Heights, with everyone standing outside on the Balgray Hill, were splashed over the front pages of all the newspapers. She had seen a couple of the papers. Betty had got them and showed them to her.

'See, there's no need to worry,' Betty assured her. 'I've checked. Look for yourself – neither you nor the children can be seen in the crowd.'

She couldn't share Betty's confidence. There were other papers in other towns. What if they could be seen in one of them? What if her husband had seen them?

Not long after she got safely into the flat, the doorbell startled her.

'It's only me,' Betty called through the letter box. Betty never used her master key to enter either of the flats without warning unless there was an emergency and it was necessary for her to rush in.

Rita looked worriedly at the woman who entered the sitting room with Betty.

'This is Kate, Rita. Kate Smythe-Bellingham.'

'Pleased to meet you,' Rita said.

Kate Smythe-Bellingham's appearance did not reflect her important-sounding, double-barrelled name. She was a small, white-haired woman, who kept avoiding eye contact.

'There's a new lady sharing with Janet and Sandra and Mary as well,' Betty said. 'Chrissie, her name is. Chrissie Cumberland. You'll meet her at the get-together tomorrow. Now, you're sharing the double bedroom with the children, Rita, so we'll put Kate in the smaller room. Where's Alice?'

'She went next door to see how wee Mary is.'

'Oh well, she'll have met Chrissie Cumberland. Chrissie arrived earlier this morning.' She turned to a helpless, confused-looking Kate. 'I'll take your case through to the bedroom, Kate. Then maybe Rita will make a cup of tea while I go and fetch Alice. Sit down and try to relax.'

Rita could have wept with the acuteness of her sympathy for the woman. She knew exactly how she was feeling.

'You'll be all right here. You'll be all right,' she repeated, not knowing what else to say. 'I'll go and put the kettle on.'

She was back in a couple of minutes carrying a tray with mugs, milk jug, sugar bowl and a plate of tea biscuits.

'Come on and I'll show you around first. It won't take a minute.'

Kate dutifully rose and followed Rita through the lobby, into the kitchen, bathroom and then the bedroom.

'We're lucky having a couple of single beds in each room and there's the bunk beds for my two. It's a bit of a squash but nothing like it used to be. Betty said in her first place, there was hardly any furniture and no beds. It was just wall-to-wall mattresses on the floor.'

Kate still hadn't said a word.

'I know how you feel, Kate. I felt the same when I first arrived. But you'll not regret it. You'll have done the right thing in leaving your man. I could bet my last dollar on that and I don't know who your man is.'

'Nobody will believe it.' Kate's voice was so quiet Rita barely caught the words.

'That's what we all think,' Rita said. 'My husband was always a right charmer outside the house. Inside . . .' she shook her head. 'I still can't talk about it.'

'My husband is a judge.'

Rita shrugged.

'So what? There's been a policeman's wife in here. And the wife of a minister of religion. You'll be meeting Janet from next door. Her husband is a company director.'

'It's so hard to believe. Sometimes I even think it must be me. I'm imagining things or it's somehow my fault.'

'Kate, Betty will tell you. She does counselling. There's a pattern to what abusers do. And that's one of the things they make you feel. That it's your fault. It takes a while to get over it, to find yourself again and to get over the fear. I'm not over it yet. Not by a long chalk. Sometimes I think I never will be. But at least I know now it wasn't my fault. There's no excuse for an abuser's behaviour. All abusers are two-faced, manipulating, power-crazy bastards. And you can't change them, no matter what you say or don't say, or do or don't do.'

There was a shout in the lobby. 'It's only me.'

'Oh, there's Betty at the door.' Rita began pouring the tea. 'Alice must have forgotten her key.'

'I was just telling Kate,' Rita added, after the necessary introductions were made, 'that all abusers are manipulating, power-mad bastards and nothing was our fault but knowing that doesn't cure our fear. I'm still terrified of the bastard I lived with.'

Betty smiled at Kate.

'Have a biscuit. Tomorrow we're having a get-together of women, some from a couple of other refuges. There's also going to be some women there who've gone through all the trauma and fear that Rita's been talking about and they've been able eventually to move on to a house of their own and a new and happy life. Meeting them and talking to them will be like seeing a light at the end of a tunnel. You won't believe just now that you'll ever be like them. It takes time, sometimes quite a long time, but just meeting women who've succeeded in overcoming their problems, just seeing that light, knowing it's possible to move a bit nearer to it, step by step as they have, will help you. Rest assured you're going to be all right.'

'That's what I told her,' Rita said.

'I can vouch for that as well,' Alice nodded eagerly, making her curls bob about. 'As long as you're inside the refuge, you're safe.'

'But he's a judge. He's got the law on his side.'

'No, he hasn't,' Betty said. 'And it doesn't matter a damn what his job is. If anything, it makes you safer here if your abuser has a respectable or important job or reputation. That type doesn't want anyone to know that they're an abuser. So they keep very quiet. Even if they found out where the wife was – which they wouldn't – they certainly would never go to any refuge to make a fuss or any kind of scene. We never have any trouble with so-called respectable professional men. So just try to relax.'

'Help yourself to milk and sugar,' Rita said. 'Have you any family?'

'A son. He's an officer in the army. I didn't want him to join the army. Before that I didn't want him to go to boarding school. But my husband insisted. Sometimes I feel I hardly know David. He went to boarding school when he was only eight. Just a little boy. Previous to that he was in a nursery.'

'Bastard!' Rita said. 'Thank God I got away before my man could separate me from my children or do them any harm.'

122

'I don't think my husband meant any harm to David. He's very proud of him.'

Just then Betty's mobile phone rang.

'Oops.' Betty stood up still holding the phone to her ear. 'A wee emergency, folks. No, nothing to do with you,' she added. 'We're always getting cries for help from some poor soul. See you tomorrow at the get-together, all right?' she added before striding away.

'Yes, OK, Betty,' Rita called after her. 'We'll look after Kate, don't worry.'

'We all look after each other here,' Alice told Kate. 'I don't know what I'd do without Rita. And I love wee Bobby and Susie.'

Kate's eyes flicked tentatively in Rita's direction.

'Where are the children just now?'

'Dorothy – that's the children's worker – has taken them and some kids from other refuges to Largs for the day.' Rita lit a cigarette and inhaled deeply. 'They'll be having a great time. Dorothy's very good with them. Always fooling about and making them laugh. Gives them a break from me. I'm always so bloody serious.'

'Och, they adore you,' Alice said. 'You're a great mum, Rita.'

'One day I'll have a house of my own somewhere.' Rita was intent on watching the smoke rise from her cigarette. 'And we'll start a new life and we'll be free of that bastard – we'll never even give him a thought.'

'I'm looking forward to the "do" tomorrow, aren't you?' Alice chewed at a biscuit. 'Especially when it means we don't have to go out.'

'What's the other new woman like?' Rita asked Alice.

'Chrissie, her name is. She's awful overweight. Huge, in fact, and she's got a whopper of a black eye. Even so, she seems much calmer and more confident than any of us. Not a bit upset. She's quite taken with wee Mary, fussing over her something awful. You know Mary,' Alice laughed. 'She's not taking kindly to that. She's been giving Chrissie up a lot of cheek. I think Chrissie must have the skin of a rhinoceros. So far, she hasn't taken a bit of offence.'

'I hope she's not the bossy type. We've all had enough of being bossed around.'

'No, not bossy but . . .' Alice hesitated. 'There's something about her. I don't quite know what it is.' Alice appeared to give herself a mental shake. 'We'll probably get on fine once we get to know her.'

20

There was a limit to the time John Ingram could stay away from his shop. He'd met a customer in Auld's Bakery and Coffee Shop, a couple of doors down from his shop – and the customer had complained about the time everybody had to wait for their cut nowadays.

'You're not the only place in Bearsden, you know,' the customer reminded him. 'You're losing customers by not being there. And it would pay you to keep an eye on things, as well as doing your share.'

So he'd tried to concentrate more on working in the shop for a time but he could not get Angela and her boyfriend out of his mind. He had decided that the red-haired man must be a boyfriend and not a husband. He'd seen him bid Angela goodnight and leave her at The Heights. If he could just find out where he lived. He'd given up the idea of getting him at the bus station. Apart from the difficulty of tracking down when he'd be there – the bastard worked shifts – the bus station was busy, day and night. Even the streets outside were always crowded. He cursed the mobs of people going into or coming out of pubs and clubs. There seemed to be no end to the amount of clubs and discos in Glasgow. Even at three o'clock in the morning, noisy crowds seethed about. How did they all manage to hold down a job? It wasn't just at weekends the clubs were packed. He couldn't understand it. He hated the revellers for the extra complication they caused him in finding, and then getting rid of, the red-haired man.

At last, and unexpectedly, his luck changed. He'd been on his way to start a new vigil at The Heights. He'd come straight from the shop, not wanting to waste another minute. He'd been working all day for several days and after spending so much time on his feet, he was glad to go upstairs every evening for a meal and a rest. This day, however, he determined he'd go straight out. He knew that if he went upstairs, once he'd had a meal, he'd just flop back in his chair and become hypnotised by television.

So he went straight from work round to the car park, got into his car and set off. Once he neared Springburn, however, he realised that he had to stop and get something to drink and a packet or two of sandwiches to keep him going for the long hours ahead of waiting and watching. It was then his luck changed. He saw the red-haired man crossing the street. John got out of his car and followed him. He was going towards the big library and sports centre building. Then suddenly he turned into a close in Kay Street. Ingram nearly went in after him but stopped himself in time.

As usual there were people about. People who could see him. People who would remember him. He wasn't some small, insignificant bloke who would easily disappear unnoticed. Despite his stoop he still looked well over six feet tall, with a body like a skeleton and a long pinched nose. He stole a quick glance in the close as he passed and saw the man veer towards the bottom flat on the right. Ingram felt like dancing back along the street to his car. He was mentally rubbing his hands in glee.

Once in the car, he tried to calm down and think how best he could get rid of the man without being seen or caught with him. Eventually he thought of a plan. It would be nothing quick and silent after all. Oh no, the red-haired bastard was going to get what he deserved. He was literally going to burn in hell.

He drove to a garage. He filled a small can with petrol. Then he drove back to Kay Street. He hid the petrol can in his large zipped holdall.

He sat for a time debating with himself whether he should wait until the place was comparatively quiet before slipping into the close. Or sneak in behind a crowd of people intent on making for the sports centre. He decided on the latter. Once in the close, he was hidden from view at the shadowy inset door of the flat. As quickly and quietly as he could, he unzipped the holdall, retrieved the petrol can, then poured the petrol through the letter box. Hands trembling with excitement, he set the petrol alight.

He controlled the impulse to run. He returned outside as quietly and surreptitiously as he had entered. Calmly, at least to all appearances, he got into his car and drove off. His luck was definitely in. The crowd had disappeared into the sports centre and, for a few vital seconds, there had been no one around to see him. His euphoria lasted all the way back to Bearsden. It wasn't until he collapsed back in his chair in the flat that he felt exhausted, then suddenly depressed.

What a fool he'd been to think that he'd succeed. OK, he wouldn't be caught. He felt secure in that knowledge. But the bastard might have escaped. It was a bottom flat. Immediately he saw the flames, the chances were he would have leapt out of the nearest window. Ingram felt sick with hatred and frustration.

It was only after lighting a cigarette and downing a stiff whisky that he began to feel better. He poured another drink. A quiver of glee returned. It might not have been possible to escape. He still might have burned in hell. Yes, he assured himself, everything was going to go his way from now on. He felt it in his bones.

Sandra was reading the *Daily Record*.

'Gosh, there's been a terrible fire in Springburn. Och, it's really horrible. The downstairs flats have been completely gutted.'

'Sandra, dear.' Chrissie pressed shovel palms over Mary's ears. 'You'll upset poor wee Mary.'

'Get yer fat paws aff ma ears,' Mary bawled. 'The only thing that upsets me is you. I'll give ye another black eye to match the wan ye've got if ye dinnae chuck it.'

Chrissie's enormous fat melted towards Mary, blotting her from view.

'Just try to relax and keep calm, darling. It's not good for you to get so excited.'

'Ah'm no' your darlin'.' Mary peered round at Sandra and Janet. 'See her, no wonder her man battered her. Ah'm itchin' tae batter her masel'.'

According to Chrissie, her husband had given her a black eye and forcibly flung her out of the house. 'But I've forgiven him,' she said kindly. The other women all thought he must have been a giant with enormous strength to have been able to accomplish such a feat. Chrissie had a long black tangle of hair that made her look like a mad witch, wee Mary said. Her face was overflowing with fat from her baggy eyes, balloon cheeks and thick lips. Tree trunks of legs bulged over boats of shoes.

Chrissie gave Mary one of what Mary called 'her smarmy smiles'.

'I know you don't mean that, darling. I'll go and make us all a nice cup of tea.' As she passed Sandra, Chrissie plucked the newspaper from her. 'There's nothing but bad news in the papers nowadays. We're better without them.'

'See her,' Mary said. 'If you two don't keep her out o' ma way, there's gonnae be a murder. Ah'm warnin' ye.'

Janet sighed. 'I hope Betty gets her a house soon.'

'Fancy her taking my paper like that.' Sandra glared furiously up through her fringe. 'Cool as a cucumber. And I was dying to know all about the fire in Springburn. I'm going to get that paper back even if I've to fight her for it.'

Mary and Janet couldn't help laughing at the ridiculous vision Sandra's words conjured up.

Janet dabbed the unaccustomed tears of hilarity from her eyes with a lace-edged hanky.

'Maybe we should speak to Betty. It might be best to wait until after tomorrow, though. She's so busy with one thing and another, including all the preparations for the get-together. There's going to be a buffet and the girls are seeing to it all by themselves.'

'Aye, well, just see that she keeps away from me. She gives me the bloody creeps.'

'We'll do our best, Mary, but she's so persistent, isn't she? And it's not as if she has a nasty manner. If she was nasty or even impolite, it might be easier for us to do something. As it is, what can we say to Betty? That she's being too nice and helpful?'

As if on cue, Chrissie filled the doorway. 'There we are with a nice cup of tea. No, don't get up, Janet. I can manage splendidly and I'm so happy to be here with such lovely people. It's a pleasure to be able to do whatever I can for all of you. Especially poor wee Mary. Can I hold the cup for you, darling?'

'God!' Mary gave a loud, heartfelt groan, making Sandra hastily pipe up, 'Mary doesn't like being fussed over, Chrissie. She likes to be independent. Don't you, Mary?'

'Aye, definitely! If you dare hold that cup up to my mouth, Chrissie Cumberland, I'll fling the bloody tea all over you. I've only one hand but believe me, it's well able to fling that tea in your face.'

'What have you done with my newspaper?' Sandra demanded dramatically. 'I was in the middle of reading it.'

'I know, dear. I heard you. What lovely red hair you have. Such a pretty little face, too.'

Sandra was absolutely infuriated. 'My hair is *not* red!'

'Whatever you say, dear.'

'There's been a terrible fire in Kay Street and I was in the middle of reading about it. What have you done with my paper?'

Janet said, 'That's near that lovely new building, isn't it? Remember, Mary, we went to the library there and got some books for everybody.' She turned to Chrissie. 'Alice next door was too nervous about going down on her own. It's an awful job to get her to put a foot outside.'

Chrissie's face melted in sympathy. 'Oh, poor Alice. I must see what I can do for her.'

'Aye,' Mary said. 'Just you forget about yours truly here and concentrate on Alice next door. She has two hands to strangle you wi'.'

'Mary doesn't mean it,' Janet said.

'It's all right, Janet,' Chrissie said. 'I forgive her and I'm sorry about your newspaper, Sandra. I only destroyed it because I didn't want you to be upset.'

Mary picked up her cup of tea and took a slurp. 'As if we hadnae enough to bother us without Saint Bloody Chrissie.'

Sandra couldn't stop thinking about what had happened. 'There must have been people killed. What a dreadful way to die – burned like that . . .'

Janet cried out in protest. 'Sandra, for pity's sake! You're upsetting me, never mind Mary. Give that imagination of yours a rest for a change.'

'Sorry. I'm terrible, aren't I?'

'Just drink yer tea,' Mary told her. 'Honest tae God, if it's no' one thing, it's another.'

Later on, after Chrissie had insisted on washing up and then making them all a cheese omelette for their supper and then washing up again, she said to Mary, 'I'll help you to undress and see you comfortably settled in bed, darling.'

Janet hastily came to Mary's rescue.

'Mary has learned to dress and undress herself and if she has any difficulty, she trusts me to help her. We're good friends now, Mary and I.'

Chrissie patted Mary's head. 'But I'm your good friend too, dear.'

'No,' Janet insisted. 'You haven't been here long enough for any of us to get to know you properly, Chrissie. These things take time. Just try to be more patient.'

'Janet, I'm the most patient of women, I can assure you, dear. I just believe, and believe most sincerely, that it's my Christian duty to do whatever I can to help, wherever I see a need. And nothing and nobody in the world will ever dissuade me from my Christian duty.'

'Oh God!' Mary groaned again.

21

Cheryl had never lived through such a nightmare. First of all, Tommy had been late in calling for her at the shop. She waited and waited. The iron frames were fixed on to the windows. The shop was locked. Still she waited. She couldn't understand it. She began to walk slowly along towards the precinct entrance. It was then she caught the frisson of excitement in the air, then the panic. People were running about outside. The wail of fire engines echoed through the precinct. She began to run. Only something terrible would have kept Tommy from meeting her tonight. Then she saw the sky was alight with an orange glare. The close in Kay Street that Tommy had described to her was burning fiercely.

'Oh no!' Cheryl screamed. 'Tommy, Tommy!' A fireman was holding her back. 'My Tommy's in there.'

'A young guy with red hair?'

'Yes, Tommy,' she screamed again. 'Tommy!'

'Calm down, hen. I don't think he's that bad. One thing's certain, though. He's quite a hero. He got the man next door out. They've both been taken to the Royal.'

She raced around the streets looking for a taxi, arms flaying and shouting like a mad thing. Usually there was a long line of black cabs at the rank just up from the sports centre but not tonight. Eventually she saw one and stepped out on to the road to flag it down.

'Have you got a death wish or something? Running out in front of me like that!'

'The Royal Infirmary, please.' She scrambled into the cab and banged the door shut. 'As quick as you can.'

'An emergency, is it?'

'There's been a fire in a house in Kay Street. My boyfriend was in it.'

'I heard the fire engines. But there's always something going on. If it's not fire engine sirens, it's the police. I've got so I don't pay any attention.'

'For God's sake, hurry up.'

'Hang on. If I go any faster, you'll end up in the hospital as a patient, not a visitor.'

Every traffic light went against them. Cheryl was perched on the edge of her seat, ready to spring out. In comparison, the driver was lounging back, apparently in complete relaxation. She even thought she heard him whistling to himself. She could have throttled him.

'There you are,' he announced cheerfully but prevented her from racing off without paying him by locking the doors until she did.

In the emergency department, she plied a nurse with desperate questions and when she eventually located Tommy, she had to control the urge to run to him and hug him, in case she caused him more pain than he must be suffering.

Despite his bandaged hands and chest and the dressing on his face, he greeted her with his usual cheeky grin.

'I'm OK, don't worry. My good jacket's ruined, though. I had to fling it over my head. I was wearing my new suit to impress you. Ah well, serves me right. Pride goes before a fall, they say.'

She kissed him carefully on the cheek.

'I hear you've been a real hero.'

'Don't be daft.'

'What on earth happened?'

It was then Cheryl saw the tragic expression in Tommy's eyes, despite his continued efforts to keep his voice light.

'Fancy, our nice wee house gone before we even had a chance to move in. Before you even set foot in it.'

'But what happened?'

'God knows. Victor, the chap next door, is still raging. He's sure somebody had it in for him. I had a devil of a job trying to haul him out the window. He kept trying to grab piles of videotapes, can you beat it? Videotapes! He nearly got us both killed.'

'I hope he wasn't raging at you.'

'Don't be daft,' Tommy repeated. 'We were both in there when the place blew up. We'd been getting on fine. He'd asked me to step in for a minute until he found the key. We were chatting away like best mates and suddenly . . . No, he's thanked me since. Even apologised that I should have been caught up in it. He said it was his problem. He has enemies and rivals, he said, and he'd find out which one of them torched the place. They'll be helluva sorry. You should have seen his face when he said that. I'm telling you, Cheryl, I wouldn't like to be in the shoes of whoever did that.'

'So it was definitely arson?'

'So it seems. The firemen and the police will be investigating the cause, I suppose, but Victor is already convinced it was somebody purposely intent on ruining him. That's what he said. He even said thousands of pounds had gone up in flames. But I think he must have been raving. He was pretty badly burned and shocked. I hardly knew what I was doing or saying myself for a while there. I mean, when I think of our wee house, Cheryl . . .'

'Och, never mind the house. There'll be other houses. It

wasn't even as if we'd signed anything or paid any rent. The important thing is you're all right, Tommy.'

'Could I ask you a favour?'

'Of course. Anything.'

'Would you go and tell my mother? Tell her not to worry. I'm fine but they want to keep me in for a few days, just to make sure.'

It was not a job Cheryl would have chosen. Nor was it something she looked forward to but she did not hesitate to agree and within half an hour, she was in another taxi and returning to Springburn.

Immediately Mrs McKechnie set eyes on Cheryl, she panicked.

'Where's my Tommy? What happened? I knew you'd bring him no luck. What have you done . . . ?'

'I haven't done anything,' Cheryl interrupted. 'And he's fine. He's in the Royal but . . .'

'He's in the Royal?' Mrs McKechnie screeched. 'He can't be fine if he's in the Royal.'

Mr McKechnie appeared then. 'What's up? Come in, hen.'

'Thanks but I'd better not.'

'She's got our Tommy into the Royal next.'

Cheryl struggled to keep calm as Mrs McKechnie grabbed a coat from a hook in the lobby.

'There was a fire at the flat.'

'I knew it! I knew no good would come of him listening to her. She's the one that talked him into that flat. Come on, you.' Mrs McKechnie punched her husband's arm. 'Fling your coat on and we'll run and get a taxi. Wait a minute till I get my purse.'

'How is he?' Mr McKechnie asked anxiously.

'Fine, fine. He said you've not to worry. They're just keeping him in for a few days so that they can change his bandages, he says. It's his chest and his . . .'

'Oh my God!' Mrs McKechnie came rushing back. 'His chest!'

Cheryl was pushed aside with a parting shot from Mrs McKechnie, 'I'll never forgive you for this. He was fine till he got mixed up with you.'

Cheryl was left standing on the landing as the couple hurried away but Mr McKechnie managed to call back, 'Sorry, hen. We'll be in touch as soon as we can.'

Not if that old harridan can help it, Cheryl thought.

Her feelings seesawed between anger and understanding. Tommy was Mrs McKechnie's only son. It was understandable that she was panicking and saying rash things she probably didn't mean. Although Cheryl couldn't quite convince herself of that. Mrs McKechnie had been polite enough in the past and had made her a nice tea when Tommy took her home. Cheryl always suspected, however, that she didn't meet with the older woman's approval.

Rain was making a fast-flowing river of the gutter when Cheryl emerged from the close. It smacked wetly over her face and made her shiver and turn up the collar of her jacket before making a run for the bus stop.

At least she hadn't to wait long for a bus. It was still bucketing down when the bus reached The Heights and she sprinted as fast as she could into the building.

'What a night,' the concierge greeted her, a cup of steaming tea clutched in one hand and his pipe in the other. 'I was speaking to your mammy earlier and she said you and your boyfriend were going to be looking at a flat. Tommy, isn't it? Nice fella.'

Cheryl shivered.

'You wouldn't believe the night I've had, Monty.'

'How? What happened, hen?'

'The flat was on fire before I even got there. Both the downstairs flats were alight and it looked as if upstairs was too.'

'Good God! Is Tommy all right?'

'He's not too bad. Bad enough, though. His chest and hands are all bandaged and he's got a dressing on his face. But he hopes to be out of hospital in a few days. A fireman told me he saved a man's life.'

'Nice fella.'

'I'd better go up and get these wet clothes off. I'm chittering.'

'Aye, on you go, hen. I'll see you tomorrow.'

There was another woman in the lift. A grossly overweight woman topped with a tangled mess of dark hair. The woman smiled at Cheryl.

'Are you all right, dear? Can I help at all?'

Cheryl stared at her as if she was mad. She'd never seen the woman before in her life.

'No, thanks.'

She turned away to press the button for floor number thirty.

'Gosh, the very top,' the woman said. 'How does it feel to be so near heaven?'

The woman was mad.

Cheryl tried to concentrate on Tommy.

'That's a very thin jacket for such wet weather, dear.' The woman was peering closely at Cheryl's jacket. 'It's clinging to your bosom and showing your nipples. And very nice nipples they are, dear.'

'Mind your own bloody business!' Cheryl cried out. This was all she needed to finish off a hellish night. A bloody creep of a woman.

'I was only giving you a compliment, dear. I'm only trying to be friendly. We are neighbours, after all.'

'Get lost. I've never clapped eyes on you before in my life.'

'Oh, but I've seen you. I'm very observant. Oh, here's my floor. I'll see you again, dear.'

Not if I see you first, Cheryl thought. Fancy, the creep must be in one of the safe houses. She'd got off at the twenty-third floor. She didn't envy the other women in there now.

She braced herself, as she stepped out of the lift, to face her mother's questions. At least her father wouldn't be back from the pub yet.

She turned her key in the lock.

'Before you say anything,' Cheryl addressed her mother in the living room, 'I'm dying for a cup of tea.'

'I've just finished mine.' Her mother's face paled with anxiety. 'But there's plenty left in the pot. Sit down and I'll fetch a clean cup.'

The tea and the chance of relaxing back in the chair beside the fire soothed her a little and she was able to tell her mother what had happened.

'Arson?' Her mother was wide-eyed with horror.

'Well, the man next door is convinced it was somebody out to get him.'

Her mother wrung her hands in agitation.

'I'm so glad it didn't come to anything.'

'What on earth do you mean?' Cheryl asked.

'Well, not getting the flat. Obviously it hasn't been a nice place with decent neighbours. That man sounds like a criminal, a gangster or something. I've heard about awful gang fights and rivalries between gangs. The papers are full of stories. Only the other day . . .'

'For pity's sake, Mammy. Tommy could have been killed.'

'Well, there you are. So could you. It doesn't bear thinking about. You're well out of there.'

'Out of where? Sharing a flat with Tommy, you mean? Well, Mammy, the first chance I get, I'll find another place and Tommy and me will move in together as we planned. And thanks for asking how he is,' she added sarcastically. 'Now, I've had one hell of a night so I'm off to bed.'

22

Janet and Sandra were both in their own bedrooms about to get ready for bed when they heard Mary scream out their names.

'Janet, Sandra!' The acute distress in the voice was unmistakable and most unusual for Mary.

They ran from their rooms to the bathroom. They knew Mary always went to the bathroom last thing at night. 'For a wee wash down.'

Mary was sitting on the toilet wearing only a short vest and the elephantine bulk of Chrissie Cumberland was bending over her.

Janet cried out, 'What do you think you're doing?'

Sandra raced over and tried to push Chrissie aside.

'I was only trying to pull poor Mary's knickers up. I could see she was struggling.'

Janet snatched up a bath towel and pushed it in front of Mary. Janet put her hand on the back of Mary's head and pressed Mary's face against her chest to hide her friend's look of distress and humiliation. The wispy hair, the bald patch, the frail trembling body enraged Janet on Mary's behalf. She glared furiously at Chrissie.

'Don't you dare come near Mary again. Don't you dare ever intrude on her privacy again.'

'The door was unlocked, dear,' Chrissie said patiently. 'I was only trying to help.'

'Well, you're not a help,' Sandra shouted. 'You're an absolute menace.'

'Yes,' Janet agreed. 'I'm going to report you to Betty first thing tomorrow. Now get out of here. Get away into your own room.'

'But I haven't done anything, dear.'

'Don't dear me. Just go.'

With a sigh, Chrissie lumbered away from the bathroom.

'It's all right, Mary,' Janet said. 'She's gone. We won't let her near you again.'

Sandra's eyes bulged dramatically. 'What a creep! None of us are safe with her on the loose. We'd better lock our bedroom doors tonight.'

'All right. All right, Sandra. Mary, do you want to manage on your own now? Or will we see you into bed?'

'Aye, aw right, hen. If ye just pal me through tae ma room, I'll be fine.'

Still holding on to Mary and her bath towel, Janet and Sandra led her back to her bedroom.

'Lock your door, Mary,' Sandra said once they reached Mary's room. 'I'm going to lock mine. That woman's a right weirdo.'

Janet sighed. 'Sandra, it's safer if Mary doesn't lock her door. We've already agreed about that. It's in case there's an emergency. How about if you slept on the other single bed in my room, Mary? Just for tonight. It would make me feel better. I wouldn't need to worry about you then.'

'Aye, OK hen. If it'll help you.' Mary visibly relaxed. Her face crumpled with gratitude as she gazed up at Janet. 'Ye're a good pal tae me, so ye are. Both of ye,' she added hastily. 'You as well, Sandra hen.'

The next day, Janet and Sandra went across to the office to

talk to Betty. It was as difficult as Janet had originally predicted. Chrissie had not done anything to break the rules. That is to say, she had not been dirty or nasty or refused to do her share of the work. On the contrary, Janet, Sandra and Mary had almost to fight to get doing their share. Nor was she nasty towards anyone. Everyone else, however, was sorely tempted to be nasty to her. The point Janet and Sandra made to Betty was Chrissie's constant intrusion into their privacy, especially into wee Mary's privacy.

'She's always touching us,' Sandra said. 'I was standing washing my dishes at the kitchen sink, for instance, and I nearly jumped out of my skin. I suddenly felt a hand slip up inside my jacket. It was her standing right up against my back. It was horrible. I was furious.'

Betty listened with her usual sympathetic attention.

Janet said, 'Yes, it's this inappropriate touching all the time. Also, although she is so big and hefty, she can move lightly and quietly and always takes us by surprise. Honestly, Betty, she is seriously upsetting wee Mary. And you know Mary. She always tries to make out she's so tough and couldn't care less. But she does care. She certainly cares about this. She's no match, physically or otherwise, for Chrissie. She's getting so upset and humiliated.'

Eventually Betty said, 'Chrissie has had a word with me earlier this morning.'

Sandra rolled her eyes. 'Oh, I know what she'd say. She was just trying to help and do her Christian duty.'

'The usual procedure is to have any complaints or problems discussed at one of our regular meetings in the head office, with the help workers from all the other refuges in the area,' Betty said. 'Don't worry, just be patient. We always do our very best to get everything sorted out, no matter what the problem is. We always try to help one another and do it in a proper democratic way.'

They had to be satisfied with that but they came away from Betty's office with renewed anger simmering underneath their polite 'thank-yous'. Anger not at Betty but at Chrissie Cumberland.

'Could you beat it? Her getting to Betty before us? Sly bitch. I can just hear her smarmy voice.' Sandra's eyes widened dramatically and her voice loudened. 'I hate that woman!'

Janet sighed. 'Let's have a cup of tea and try to calm down. I'm sure Betty and the other workers will do their best.'

'Where's wee Mary?' Sandra suddenly cried out.

'Now, do try to keep calm, Sandra. Mary was going to have a long lie in bed. We'll take her through a cup of tea.'

'I'm going to run through and check on her. She's been in the house alone with that weirdo while we've been in Betty's office.'

Janet sighed again. Sandra was so excitable at times.

Still, she could not help feeling a sudden twinge of anxiety herself.

★★★★★

Ingram felt as if he was drowning. Fear kept welling up over his head.

The papers reporting on the fire were now saying that the man who lived in one of the downstairs flats had been badly burned on the face and body. His age was given as fifty-two. Victor O'Donnell, fifty-two years of age. The red-haired man was much younger than that. Apparently O'Donnell was a suspected drug dealer and it was thought that the arsonist could be a rival of his. Traces of heroin and crack cocaine had been found in the ruins and a rumour was going around that O'Donnell had lost a fortune and had sworn to track down whoever had torched the place.

There was also a report about the bravery of twenty-one-year-old Tommy McKechnie who had saved O'Donnell's life.

Ingram kept having to wipe his brow and face. He wasn't just sweating with fear. He was seething with fury and frustration. But fear was the strongest emotion. He tried to think back to the scene, to remember every move he'd made. His mind strained to picture everything exactly. Had there been anybody there who could have seen him? There definitely had not been anyone in the immediate vicinity of the close.

But had there been any lit windows in the street? Could someone have been looking out of a window? He hadn't thought about that at the time. He daren't think of what might happen to him if this Victor O'Donnell found out he was responsible for his injuries and the destruction of his home and the fortune in drugs that might have been inside. It was a nightmare. Ingram kept trembling at the thought. But surely no one had seen him. Oh, how fervently he prayed that no one had seen him.

Then another terrifying thought occurred to him. He had bought a can of petrol from a garage not a mile from the place. Would anyone remember him from there and connect him with the fire?

He did not go to work all day. Nor did he venture anywhere else. He remained shut up in his flat. Hardly daring to move. He'd wait. He'd wait for days, weeks if necessary, until he was certain that it was safe to go out. After a few days, his food ran out and his milk and his cigarettes. Self-consciously, neck elongated, head pushing forward, eyes down, he left the flat and went to Auld's Bakery for his usual sandwiches. He also collected several newspapers and packets of cigarettes. Back at the house, he devoured every word of every newspaper before he even made a cup of coffee or lit a cigarette. There was not one word about the fire, or about Victor O'Donnell. Gradually, relief began to soothe his tensed-up nerves.

'Thank God! Thank God!' he repeated out loud.

Of course no one had seen him. He had made sure of that, hadn't he? As far as the petrol was concerned, the man whom he'd paid for his purchase never even gave him a glance. He remembered now.

Thank God! Thank God!

He made a cup of coffee, lit a cigarette and opened one of the packets of sandwiches.

He felt almost happy. Eventually curiosity got the better of him. How was Angela taking all that had happened to her boyfriend Tommy, he wondered? Tommy, the local hero. Bitterness returned to twist his mouth. He picked up the phone.

'Angela?'

'John! I thought I'd never hear from you again. I thought you must have forgotten about me.' Oh, that lovely lilt in her voice. What a torment it was to him.

'No, no.'

'I hope you've been well enough. There's so much flu going around.'

'No, I've just been busy during the day and then tired at night. I've been watching television and reading the newspapers. By the way, I hope you're all right. You don't live near where that awful fire was, do you?'

'What fire?'

'In Springburn.'

Her voice slowed down with wariness.

'I don't live in Springburn. What made you think I did?'

'You must have mentioned something that made me think that. Or was it someone you know who lives in Springburn? Maybe that's why I thought . . .'

'No. I don't know anyone in Springburn. I couldn't have said anything like that.'

'Oh, I'm sorry. So you're fine then?'

'Yes, I'm perfectly all right, John.'

'Good, good.'

By God, she was a good actress.

'I was hoping you'd changed your mind about meeting me, Angela. I feel so lonely at times. Do you never feel lonely?'

Her voice saddened. He was sure he recognised genuine sadness.

'Yes, I do,' she sighed. 'Indeed I do, John.'

'Well, then. Angela, for God's sake, tell me the truth. Why do you keep . . . ?'

'I'm sorry, John. I must ask you not to phone me again. I'm going to have my name withdrawn from the agency. Goodbye.'

He stared at the now silent phone.

'Oh no,' he said. 'Not that way.'

23

Mabel wept. It had been so painful saying goodbye to John. Her dear friend. Her first and only love. She wandered about the house hardly knowing what she was doing, not caring, not seeing anything except a wet shimmer. Eventually, exhausted, she collapsed back into the chair, took off her spectacles and, with a trembling hand, tried to dry the glass with a paper hanky. She replaced her spectacles on the bridge of her nose and stared around the room. What an ugly claustrophobic place it was with its dark, overpowering furniture, its heavy brown plush curtains and fringed table cover and the monotonous tick-tock of the clock. The ghosts of her mother and father were with her here in the room, were always there, had never left. They were pressing down on her, suffocating her, depressing her just as they had always done. Panic fountained up, threatening to swirl her into reckless action, like running from the room, far away from the building, far away from Balornock and Springburn. It was only a desperate, crazy vision, however. It only darkened her cloud of depression.

She could hardly walk, far less run. Anyway, where could she go? Mixed in with all her other emotions was the pain of having abandoned John, of having caused him pain. He suffered loneliness and depression too. He had told her that more than once. How must he be feeling now? He loved her. At least he loved Angela, the beautiful young woman that he thought she was. She wished now that before she said her final goodbye, she had blurted out the truth.

'I'm so sorry, John,' she should have said. 'I've been lying to you. Everything has been a lie. I'm not young. I'm not beautiful. I'm not even called Angela. I'm an ugly, crippled old woman called Mabel.'

But even if she'd had the courage to say all of these things, it would probably only have made everything worse. As well as the loneliness, he would have suffered shock. He would have been horrified, not only at what she'd told him but at the cruelty of her continuing deception. Angry too, no doubt.

She felt so ashamed. He was only a young man, a mere thirty-nine years of age, young enough to be her son. She couldn't bear to sit another moment in the silent house with so many dreadful thoughts and memories tormenting her. She caught hold of her stick and heaved herself to her feet.

She still had some money left. She'd take the bus into town and have one last treat to cheer her up. She'd window shop. She'd visit Marks & Spencer's food department and buy something nice for her supper. Then she'd go across Sauchiehall Street to the Willow Tea Rooms, her favourite place to have afternoon tea.

A gale was whistling down the Balgray Hill when she emerged from The Heights. For a few minutes at least, her mind had been diverted from her own problems by the gossip she overheard going down in the lift.

Poor Cheryl Patterson was in an awful state. She was telling the girl from the refuge – the one with the glossy hair and the fringe that hung down over her brows, Sandra her name was – that Tommy, Cheryl's boyfriend, had been badly burned in a fire in Kay Street in Springburn. She was on her way to visit Tommy in the hospital.

Apparently it was a case of arson. Most of the people in the upstairs flats had been out at work. Only one elderly woman had been at home and she was in hospital suffering from smoke inhalation, as well as burns. The person in the other bottom flat had suffered worse burns than Tommy. Tommy had saved the man's life. Somebody had tipped off the newspapers that the man was a drug dealer.

'And you'll never guess,' Cheryl said as they left the lift and went across the hallway. 'Drugs were found in the sleeves of video tapes and behind sockets in the walls. Electrical sockets! Fancy! And as well as behind the sockets . . .'

Mabel lost the rest of the conversation because Cheryl and Sandra reached the door and disappeared outside.

Once outside herself, Mabel had to grip as tightly as she could to her stick and concentrate on keeping her balance. She suddenly feared that a time would come when she would not be able to venture out at all. Then what would she do? How would she survive? She wished she lived in a refuge or 'safe house', as it was also called. What a lovely name. *Safe house*. How wonderful to feel safe and looked after by someone strong and capable like Betty, the safe house worker. She'd often seen Betty in the lift. Most people completely ignored Mabel, especially the young people who lived in The Heights. But not Betty. Betty always smiled at her and said good morning. On a few occasions she had even chatted to Mabel. Betty was a lovely big woman. There was such a reassuring firmness about her, yet a caring warmth too. It must be like heaven living in the safe house.

Mabel had a terrible struggle getting on to the bus. Bus platforms were so high. The driver or one of the other passengers always had to help her on and guide her into a seat. She was getting worse, more helpless, by the day. There was no doubt about it. The realisation made her feel frightened. Getting off the bus at the Buchanan Bus Station was another ordeal. She needed a lot of help with that too. She could have wept with helplessness and frustration. Again it took a good deal of effort and concentration to negotiate her way to Sauchiehall Street. Today what added to her distress was the sight of a couple of gaudy-coloured and noisy fairground machines. On one, children were strapped into a line of seats and then the machine shot high in the air, up and down, up and down, with music blaring and children screaming. The other was a circle of model cars and trains in which the children sat, gripping steering wheels and pretending to drive as the roundabout trundled round and round, again to the loud blare of music.

It increased Mabel's sadness. What a difference to the beautiful, distinguished Sauchiehall Street that had once been world famous as a high-class shopping centre. Daly's, Pettigrew & Stephens, Copeland & Lye – Mabel remembered them all. Now it was mostly all cheap places aimed at teenagers. She was thankful that at least the Willow Tea Rooms was still there. It no longer extended over five levels as it used to but it was still a beautiful place with its original Charles Rennie Mackintosh designs. From its outset, the Room de Luxe was the main attraction with its silver furniture, leaded mirror friezes and wooden lattice-type screens fixed to the walls.

The only drawback as far as Mabel was concerned was the flight of stairs she had to climb. There was now a jewellery shop on the ground floor and it glittered and sparkled her way towards the stairs. As usual, because the place was so popular, especially with tourists, she had to wait in a queue. However, it was worth it in the end. The waitresses in their black dresses and little white aprons were all so pleasant and helpful and the tea and cakes were absolutely delicious. Mabel gratefully savoured each sip and crumb.

She knew, in every aching bone of her body, that this would be the last time she would be either physically or financially able to enjoy such a luxurious treat.

The 'afternoon tea' was served on a three-tiered silver cake stand holding sandwiches, scones, a little dish of butter, another of cream and another of jam. There was also a plate of mouthwatering cakes. The tea came in a silver pot with a tea strainer, a little receptacle for the strainer and a milk jug and sugar bowl. Not forgetting a dainty napkin.

Mabel made everything last as long as possible. As well as the meal, she enjoyed watching the other diners, especially the tourists, who busied themselves taking photographs of the place. Charles Rennie Mackintosh had been, and still was, famous all over the world.

Eventually, with reluctance and regret, Mabel struggled to her feet, paid her bill and, slowly, carefully, hanging on to the banister, returned downstairs, through the silver, gold and diamond sparkle, and out on to noisy Sauchiehall Street.

Litter flapped around her. She saw a woman, followed by two young children, all eating some kind of fast food from a paper tray, actually toss the tray on to the pavement. Mabel was shocked. What an example to give to children – especially when there was a rubbish bin only a few feet away.

What was the world coming to? What was Glasgow coming to? At least if you looked up, you could still see the lovely architecture of the place. Only, her sight was so poor now that she found it difficult to see anything very clearly. She was beginning to have a problem even deciphering the numbers on buses once she returned to the bus station.

Back at The Heights, she struggled into the foyer. She managed to smile at Monty, the concierge, who was sitting as usual with his door open so that he could see everyone coming and going. He liked to keep abreast of all the gossip too.

He did not usually speak to her, knowing no doubt that nothing interesting ever happened to her. Today, however, he was obviously bursting to talk to someone, anyone.

'Afternoon, Miss Smith,' he called.

She smiled at him again.

'Have you heard about Cheryl? You know, the blonde lassie on the thirtieth floor?'

Mabel was confused for a moment. 'Something's happened to Cheryl?'

'No, her boyfriend.'

'Oh, yes. The fire. What a terrible thing.'

'A drug dealer as well. What do you bet there's going to be a gang war starts as a result of that fire?'

'I do hope not,' Mabel said nervously. She was thinking of the crowds of youths always hanging about outside The Heights. She'd heard somebody say that they were 'into drugs'.

'You mark my words,' Monty said.

In a few minutes, she was in the lift and then the oppressive darkness of the house enveloped her. The silence now seemed ominous, threatening. She felt more alone and frightened than ever. She double-checked that she'd locked the door. Indeed, each time she passed to go to the bathroom or into the kitchen to make a cup of cocoa or to fill her hot water bottle, she felt compelled to check again. She looked in every room, too. She wished the three bedrooms each had a lock so that she could lock them from the outside. And the kitchen and the living room. She became obsessive about everything.

Before she went to bed, she checked the outside door and every room yet again. Then she checked that she had turned each tap off properly and that she had remembered to switch off all the lights. Then she felt afraid of the darkness in the bedroom. She switched on the bedside lamp but her eyes kept being fearfully drawn towards the bedroom door. She tried to reason with herself. She was being neurotic and ridiculous. She knew it. Who could possibly get into the house? Who would even want to?

24

Cheryl sat beside Tommy's hospital bed, holding his hand.

'Monty says there's going to be a gang war.'

'Och, what does Monty know? He's a right old blether.'

'Still, if there's drugs involved – and according to all the papers, there is – I wouldn't be a bit surprised. I'm just worried in case you get involved.'

'Don't be daft. All I did was go in to get the key.'

'But you saved the guy.'

'Well, so what?'

'One of his rivals might think it was because you're one of his lot!'

Cheryl was near to tears. It was distressing enough looking at Tommy's burned face and bandaged chest, without worrying about what other terrible things might happen to him.

'Now, why would anyone think that? It's been in all the papers that I just called for the key of the flat next door. I'd never seen the man before in my life.'

The dressing had been removed from Tommy's face but his skin still looked red, raw and painful. He seemed his usual cheerful self, though.

'And don't worry about losing the flat.' Tommy squeezed her hand. 'We'll get another, better flat. I promise.'

She nodded and made an effort to control her urge to crumple forward and weep.

He grinned at her. 'The worst that's happened as far as I'm concerned is that my face is now as red as my hair and I've always hated my ginger nut.'

'I love your hair.'

Tommy rolled his eyes. 'You *are* daft. Give us a kiss. But be gentle with me.'

Cheryl couldn't help smiling. Then, gently, lovingly, she kissed his lips.

'Your face'll heal OK. I asked the nurse. So don't you worry. And you'll soon be out of here. I'll keep looking for flats. I'll go straight after this visiting hour to view the couple I showed you in the paper.'

'Yes, the one in Anniesland sounds good. Anniesland's a nice area. On the way to Bearsden as well. One day we might even make enough cash between us to live out in Bearsden.'

Cheryl made a face. 'A right snobby place, I've heard. I don't fancy it, do you?'

'Not really. It's a bit far out. Anniesland would do us fine. Nice red sandstone houses. But the Byres Road one would be great as well.'

'Both are nice and near the shops.'

'Let me know what you think as soon as you've seen them.'

'I won't even wait until tomorrow's visiting time. I'll phone in a message.'

'I'll keep my fingers crossed.'

She had to tear herself away because the nurse came to remind her that the visiting time was over.

She took the bus from town along Great Western Road and got off to see the Byres Road flat first. Anniesland was a good bit further along Great Western Road. Right away she liked the Byres Road area. She had read something about it, of course. As soon as she'd seen the advert, she'd rushed to buy one of the slim paperbacks about the different areas of Glasgow. So far, she hadn't seen one about Anniesland and all the little publications were more about the past history of the areas than the present. But the Byres Road booklet had given her some idea of the place. It maybe was not as posh as Bearsden but Cheryl thought it was far more interesting.

Apparently it was when the University of Glasgow moved from the High Street to the West End that Byres Road had become one of the busiest and most popular streets. Like so many places in Glasgow, it was a hilly area. Originally, the houses in the aptly named Hillhead had been built for the city's wealthy businessmen. Gradually, however, the big houses were split into flats. The nearness of the university and the BBC attracted lots of writers and artists, as well as students.

Cheryl still thought wistfully of how she would love to have been a student at the university. She'd never admitted this to anyone, not even to Tommy, in case she'd be laughed at. But oh, how often, in her secret dreams, she'd escaped from The Heights and from the Springburn shopping centre and become a student living in the university campus. Unlike most of her contemporaries, she had actually enjoyed school. If it had not been for her father continuously squandering all his wages on drink, she could easily have gone on to pass her exams and gain a place at the university. Instead, however, she had had to leave school and start slaving away, earning cash to help pay for the rent in The Heights. She hated the place and would be oh so glad to get out of it.

Byres Road would be further away from both The Heights and Springburn. She wouldn't even miss Springburn Park because here, on Great Western Road, just across from the top end of Byres Road, was the Botanic Gardens with its fascinating Kibble Palace full of tropical trees, plants and elegant statues. Much of the material for classwork in the Botany Department of the university was supplied from the Kibble Palace.

Across from one side of the park was the building that housed the BBC. Cheryl thrilled at the thought of all the actors and actresses and other famous people who would work there. No doubt, if she got the flat in Byres Road, she'd see these people in the many restaurants, pubs and cafés in Byres Road.

The flat that was advertised to let was situated above some shops in a red sandstone building near the top end of the street. Cheryl could imagine herself enjoying sitting at the window gazing down at everybody milling about. She and Tommy could pass their free time having coffee in one of the cafés or strolling in the Botanic Gardens in the summer. She prayed that she would get the flat.

The rent was a bit steep, very steep actually. She could never have afforded it on her own but with Tommy's wages as well . . . And after all, it was fully furnished and it had a bathroom.

It was just as good as she had hoped – better even. It had a nice big hall, a huge kitchen with a dining area, a large sitting room, a double bedroom and all with high, ornate corniced ceilings. Not only was there a bath in the bathroom but a shower as well. Bliss!

She knew right away that it was the one. She had taken the day off to visit Tommy in the early afternoon and, because she had managed to arrive before anyone else (who no doubt would only be able to view the flat in the evening), she was successful. She felt like dancing all the way back down the stairs. The only drawback was that the entry date was not until the end of the month. That meant over three weeks yet to be stuck at home. Nevertheless, she could hardly wait to phone the hospital.

She wasn't going to visit Tommy in the evening because his mum and dad were going to be there. They had insisted, or at least Mrs McKechnie had insisted, that they wanted to be on their own with Tommy when they visited him. They wanted to have Tommy all to themselves. The real reason they went in the evening was of course because they knew she worked every day except Sunday and normally wouldn't be able to see Tommy during the day. Mrs McKechnie would think it was a good way to separate her from Tommy. Certainly she couldn't take every afternoon off. The next time she'd manage would be Sunday. Meantime, there was the joyous phone call to tell Tommy that they'd got a flat – a beautiful, wonderful flat. They couldn't move in immediately but it was well worth waiting for.

Her mother was obviously trying to feel happy for her.

'I'm so glad for your sake, hen.' She nodded as if trying to convince herself. 'If you're happy, that's enough for me.'

'Thanks, Mammy.' Cheryl hugged her. 'I'll come back regularly for visits and you'll visit me and it'll be great.'

Her mother nodded several times again and Cheryl added, 'It's not as if Byres Road is away at the other end of the world. The West End is less than half an hour from here in the bus.'

Nod, nod.

Cheryl felt sorry for her mother but there was nothing more she could do. She'd done all she could for as long as she could. Time to move on and out. Time for her father to get a grip of himself and go to AA or do something, anything, to stop himself ruining his own life, as well as everyone else's.

Soon she would have the key. The key of her own flat. The key of the flat that will be our home, she thought joyously.

She couldn't wait to tell everyone. Even the ancient old thing she often saw in the lift. Miss Smith, Monty said her name was.

'You'll never guess, Miss Smith,' she cried out on the way down to tell Alice and Rita and everyone else, including Monty, 'I've got a lovely flat in the West End. Byres Road. I'm so happy. I'll be leaving here in about three weeks' time.'

'That's nice, dear,' Miss Smith said. She had an unusual lilting voice, surprisingly young sounding. Not like a Glasgow voice at all. 'I'm so happy for you.'

'I don't think you've met my Tommy. He's a lovely man, kind and generous. A man in a million. I feel so lucky.'

'I think I have seen him. A red-haired young man?'

'That's him.'

'Treasure him, my dear.'

'Oh I will. I will. He's in hospital just now but he'll be getting out soon. Did you hear about the fire in Kay Street?'

'Yes, it was on the news on television. What a dreadful thing to happen and I believe they suspect arson.'

'Yes, it was. Fancy! It was just as well we didn't get that flat in Kay Street. The guy next door was a drug dealer.'

Miss Smith tutted. Then she said, 'So you'll be leaving here in a few weeks' time?'

'I'd like to go right now, this minute, but of course I've lots to do first. For one thing, I'm going to try and find a job over in the Byres Road area. I saw a few adverts in shop windows. I don't think I'll have any bother.'

Miss Smith sighed. 'I'll miss you.'

Cheryl nearly laughed. It was so odd. She'd never even spoken to the old woman before in her life. Perhaps a nod of recognition, maybe the occasional 'good morning'. That was all.

Now she felt guilty at not having spoken to her before. Maybe the old thing was lonely. She left Miss Smith at the twenty-third floor so that she could visit her friends in the refuge flats. She was feeling quite sorry for Miss Smith. She looked so ancient, so pathetic, with her shaking, bent figure, thick pebble glasses and gnarled hands gripping a metal hospital stick.

Once out of the lift, however, and with the lift doors closed behind her, Cheryl's joy swooped her spirits heavenwards again.

She rattled on the letter box of the safe house door.

Safe house! That's what the Byres Road house will be for Tommy and me, she thought. *Safe house!*

157

25

There was a meeting at the Women's Help head office and also a meeting between the women at both flats in The Heights refuge. At the meeting, Betty and Dorothy listened to all the complaints while Chrissie Cumberland sat smiling with apparent happy contentment. All of the women – wee Mary, Janet, Sandra, Alice, Rita and even Kate Smythe-Bellingham – found this totally infuriating. All had complaints of intrusions of privacy and inappropriate touching but nothing seemed to touch Chrissie Cumberland.

Eventually, encouraged by Betty to speak up, Chrissie announced that she had bumped into an old neighbour during one of her many excursions into town.

'You'll never guess.' Chrissie smiled around at everyone. 'She told me my Joey has had a stroke and is in hospital. So of course I'm going to go back and look after the dear man. I've arranged for him to be brought home from hospital. He's quite helpless, poor darling.'

The sympathy for poor Joey about to be at the mercy of Chrissie was a horror evident on every face. The horror was so strong, it was palpable in the very air of the room.

Eventually Betty managed, 'Oh, right. When exactly do you plan to leave then, Chrissie?'

Chrissie favoured them all with yet another smile. Then her kindly stare rested on Betty.

'I'm all packed and ready. So could you phone for a taxi for me, darling?'

'Yes, of course,' Betty assured her. 'I'll do it right away.'

And so it was that Chrissie Cumberland left the refuge. But not before each woman had to grit her teeth and suffer being pressed against Chrissie's sweating flesh in a slow bear hug.

Betty made a cup of tea for everyone after Chrissie had gone.

'Thank God!' Sandra made an ungainly flop back in her chair, legs outstretched. 'If my husband was alive, she was enough to have made me go back to him.'

'Don't be stupid,' Rita said. 'Your man was a murdering bastard.'

'Sandra's no' stupid,' wee Mary piped up defensively. 'I know what she meant. You hadn't to put up wi' Chrissie as much as we had. Ah don't know what I'd have done without Sandra. An' Janet as well. I'll no' have you or anybody else sayin' wan word against either o' them.'

'All right, all right.' Rita raised her hands in mock submission. 'No need to get your knickers in a twist.'

Dorothy poured the tea and Betty strode around the room, handing out steaming mugs. Then she offered everyone a chocolate biscuit.

'Relax everybody. Problem solved.'

Sandra gazed tragically up from under her fringe. 'But think of poor Joey.'

'We've enough to worry about in our own lives, Sandra,' Janet said. 'We can't take on the world's problems.'

'All I hope,' wee Mary said, 'is that he'll get better and give her another black eye.'

It took them the rest of the day to relax properly. Or at least to relax as much as was possible in the circumstances.

They felt relatively safe in the refuge. But overshadowing their lives was always the fear that their husbands or partners would one day discover where they were and come after them – as Sandra's husband had done. Or if they ventured out, they would be seen and forced back into a life of violence and abuse.

Alice was still terrified to put a foot outside the building. However, there had been a few occasions recently when either Rita or Sandra, or Janet or wee Mary, had persuaded her to come with them, firstly down to Springburn and then right into the centre of the city. Alice had walked between them all the time, hanging tightly on to them. She believed that her husband, knowing that she would be in the Springburn Park area, would still be somewhere around. It was the beginning of November now and there was Christmas shopping to start thinking about and Christmas cards to be bought. Although no one could afford very much or had much heart for the festive season.

Nevertheless Betty and Dorothy insisted on hanging up Christmas decorations.

'For the children's sake,' Dorothy said. And for the children's sake they tried very hard not to be frightened.

Janet hadn't the heart to tell Mary to return to her own bedroom after Chrissie left and so Mary's few belongings were moved into Janet's room.

*****

Although it was only mid-afternoon, it was dark. Not only that, a ghostly mist spread across the whole city, completely blotting it out. The Heights, with every window lit, seemed to float like a tall ship in a sea of cold blackness.

Mabel shivered. She fervently wished she had never ventured out. But she had no milk or bread or margarine left in the house. Her porridge oats were finished as well. How could she face another day without her porridge and milk for breakfast? It wasn't far to the small local supermarket. This was what she was reduced to. She could not afford, nor was she able, to go into town and trail about the busy city streets. Carefully she shuffled along, using her stick to feel her way forward. She couldn't see more than a couple of yards at most in front of her. Even the air inside the store was grey and damp.

She saw Betty from the refuge with a trolley full of all sorts of groceries but Betty didn't notice her at the back of the queue. Not for the first time, Mabel wished she was one of the refuge women and was under Betty's strong, protective wing. She longed for the company of the women in the two refuge flats and at the social events in the meeting room. How fortunate these women were to have found such a place. Mabel struggled back to The Heights with her shopping bag dangling awkwardly over her arm.

'Hello there, Miss Smith,' Monty greeted her. 'Some pea souper, eh?'

'Yes. There's usually such a wonderful view between the buildings of the whole of Glasgow, isn't there? But it's completely disappeared.'

'Aye, real creepy, isn't it?'

She nodded in agreement. She was reluctant to continue across to the lift and return to her silent, empty flat. It could be described as 'creepy' as well. Monty had returned his attention to his *Daily Record*, however, and she couldn't think of anything else to say. The lift sped her up to the twenty-fifth floor. There she was forced to cross the dismal, graffiti-covered landing and go into her flat. She switched on all the lights.

She thought longingly of John. What would he be doing just now, she wondered? In one of his conversations, when he was desperately pleading for her to meet him, he had assured her that she had nothing to fear. He was a respectable businessman with a lovely home in Bearsden. *Bearsden*, he emphasised. Oh, how she longed to be with him in beautiful, leafy Bearsden. Her parents used to have a friend there and she had accompanied her mother and father on visits to Bearsden several times. It was a place, she remembered, of beautiful villas and tree-lined streets. It was indeed a very respectable place and she had no doubt whatsoever that John was a perfectly respectable man.

As she hobbled about in the kitchen putting her few purchases away and filling the kettle, she wept. Right now, she would have gladly done anything to be as young and beautiful as Cheryl Patterson up there on the thirtieth floor. Bitterness overcame her as she carried her cup of tea into the dark brown cave of a sitting room. It even smelled of age and decay. In desperation, she switched on the television. It could give the illusion of company. Yet, it couldn't stop her from weeping.

It was a long time before it occurred to her that there might be one way to feel closer to John. If she took the bus to Bearsden, made a morning or an afternoon of the visit and had a cup of tea in Drymen Road. A cup of tea wouldn't cost much. She remembered there was a café in a baker's shop in Drymen Road. At least she would be nearer to John there than here, sitting alone in a high-rise flat on the Balgray Hill. She would be breathing the same air as John. She could sit at the window of the café watching the passers-by in the hope that she might even see John. Didn't she have his description – very tall and thin with a long nose?

She told herself she was being foolish. Nevertheless, she felt a definite lift to her spirits and was grateful for it.

And after all, what was the harm?

26

'Oh Tommy, it could have been you!' Mrs McKechnie wrung her hands in distress. 'That old woman was just up the stairs from where you were in that house in Kay Street and now she's dead. It was in this morning's paper.'

Tommy sighed. He had invited Cheryl to come for a meal with him on the evening he'd got home from hospital. He'd thought that would be all right now that he was a lot better. Obviously he had been mistaken.

'But it *wasn't* me, Mum.'

'If you had never been there, you would never have been in any danger. This was all your idea.' Mrs McKechnie turned on Cheryl. 'Tommy was perfectly happy in his own home here with me and his daddy.'

'No, you mustn't blame Cheryl, Mum. I had already made up my mind that at twenty-one, it was time I branched out on my own. It had nothing to do with Cheryl.'

'I don't care what you say, Tommy. I believe . . .'

'Well, don't.' Tommy's voice strained with impatience. 'And I've news for you. We've got another flat. A better flat. Not in Springburn. In Byres Road.'

'Away in the West End? I bet you anything . . .' Mrs McKechnie cried out.

But Mr McKechnie interrupted her. 'Great, son. It's really nice over there. I hope the pair of you will be very happy.'

'Thank you, Mr McKechnie.' Cheryl spoke up for the first time. 'It's a really nice flat. I hope you and Mrs McKechnie will come and visit us there.'

Mrs McKechnie's mouth hardened into silence. The rest of the meal was eaten with only the occasional attempt at conversation by Tommy, his father and Cheryl. It was a terrific relief to Cheryl when they eventually said their goodbyes. She was shaken by the news that a woman had died in the fire. To some degree, she felt the same as Mrs McKechnie. It could so easily have been Tommy. They clung to each other all the way along the street, her arm around his waist and his encircling hers.

'I wish we could be going home to our lovely Byres Road flat just now instead of you taking me back up to The Heights.'

'It won't be long now. We'll be nicely settled in time for Christmas.'

'Will we put decorations up?'

'Of course.'

'And have a tree?'

'Definitely.'

'Oh, Tommy. I can just imagine it. We'll be so happy.'

She leaned her head against him and, as they walked along, they planned everything they'd do to the flat. As well as the Christmas decorations, they'd hang up pictures. It was classy to have paintings on the walls. They both liked Jack Vettriano and, when they could afford it, they might get prints. They weren't too expensive. Some of his paintings were very sexy.

They would have preferred an unfurnished flat and had everything to their taste but they hadn't been able to find an unfurnished place. Maybe if they'd given themselves more time but the truth was they couldn't bear to wait. They were willing to take anything, anywhere, as long as they could be together.

'At least the furniture's modern-looking, although it's a bit scuffed,' Tommy said.

'Don't worry, cream cushions will cover any of the worn bits.'

'Brilliant! Cream against the black. That'll look real classy.'

'And I thought a cream rug instead of that brown one.'

'Great!'

'Fancy having a piano there. I've never seen a house that had a piano in it before, have you?'

'A bloke upstairs from Mum has a keyboard. How about if we both took piano lessons and learned to play duets?'

Cheryl did a little bounce of excitement.

'I'd love it. I'd love it.'

It suddenly occurred to her that now she could do anything, learn anything. Neither her mother nor her father could hold her back any more. There was the Open University. That way she could study at home when Tommy was on late shift. Perhaps he'd be interested in doing an Open University course too. Then they could study together. She knew he was a great reader. He loved books. He'd been going to the library since he was a wee boy, he'd told her. It was one of the things she admired about him. He didn't need to go to pubs. He didn't need to drink or take drugs. He didn't need props or escape routes. He had character. And ambition. He wouldn't always be a bus driver. She wouldn't always be a shop girl. They were going places together. She knew it. She was so deliriously happy, she felt she could die of it.

*****

Kate Smythe-Bellingham was trying to look calm. The other women could see by the light in her eyes that she was relieved and happy.

'Well,' Betty said. 'It's your decision. I just hope you know what you're doing, Kate.'

'My son assured me his dad was really, truly sorry. My husband actually admitted to David what he'd done. He'd been under a lot of strain with his job, he explained. I met David in town. He's been on leave. He said he believed his dad is really sorry and he wants to make it up to me. He's promised that he'll never behave like that again. He'll never be violent to me again. David said he was naturally shocked when he heard what his dad had done, but he really believes that he regrets it and that he'll keep his promise and I'll be all right.'

Rita rolled her eyes. 'Promises, promises.'

'He *has* been under a lot of strain,' Kate said. 'He has a very responsible job. He's a judge.'

'Aye,' wee Mary's voice was sarcastic, 'so you've told us, hen.'

Sandra leaned forward. 'So you're actually going back into the lion's den? Well at least you know how to escape and where to come to now.'

'I know my husband,' Kate said proudly. 'He is a man of honour and if he gives his word, then he'll keep it.'

'Right,' Betty repeated. 'As I say, it's your decision, Kate, but rest assured, Women's Help is always here if you need it.'

Afterwards, when Betty had returned to her office and Kate had gone to her room to pack, the others took bets on whether or not she would be back.

'I do hope she'll be all right,' Janet said. 'You never know. He might be a man of honour, as she says.'

'I bet the next time she leaves home, it'll be on a stretcher.'

'Trust you, Sandra.' Alice shook her head. 'You're always such a ray of sunshine.'

'Huh, look who's talking.'

'I bet no one in Newton Mearns suspects a thing,' Janet

said. 'It'll be much the same as Bearsden. No one will believe Kate. That's the worst of it. I knew no one would believe me. That's why I never even confided in the other ladies in the church. Especially the ladies in the church.'

'It's not surprising, when you think of it,' Sandra said. 'I mean, Newton Mearns and Bearsden are such posh places. Especially Newton Mearns. Everybody always takes it for granted that it's drunken, working-class men who beat their wives, never anyone living in a respectable place with a respectable job.'

'Ah well,' Janet sighed. 'We live and learn.'

Kate came to say goodbye to everyone before she left. Her face was shimmering with excitement.

'Oh, I'm so looking forward to returning to my own lovely home. It's such a relief to know it's all over and I can get back to normal. Not that I haven't been comfortable here,' she added hastily. 'But there's nothing like one's own bed and one's own fireside, is there?'

Rita rolled her eyes after Kate had gone. She mimicked the polite voice.

'There's nothing like one's own bed and one's own fireside. Silly cow. I'll give her two weeks, three at most.'

'Poor soul,' Janet sighed again. 'It took me a long time . . . Oh well, never mind. I'm all right now.'

'*I* don't feel all right,' Alice said.

'Nor me,' Sandra echoed. 'My life's ruined.'

'You're lucky,' Rita said. 'Your man's dead, Sandra. What have you got to complain about?'

'His parents have moved into what was my home. They blame me for what happened. They told that to the newspapers. He was a good boy before he met me, they said. I must have driven him to it, they said.'

'So, you'll get another house. Why should you care what they say?'

'Yes,' Alice agreed. 'You're all right, Sandra. I live in constant fear that my husband'll find me. I wish *he* was dead.'

'It's time you stopped thinkin' like that, hen,' Mary said. 'You're doin' yourself no good. You're ruinin' your own life, just as I ruined my own life wi' the drink.'

'Yes,' Janet agreed. 'We've all got to be brave and try to think positively.'

Rita's laughter had a sarcastic ring to it. 'I bet you'd be the first person to go to bits if your precious company director turned up.'

'Here you, don't talk to my pal like that. She's been braver than you and she's been out and about more than any of us. So just less o' your cheek.' Then to Janet, 'Never mind her, hen. He's no' goin' tae turn up. Don't you worry.'

Janet got up. 'I'll go and put the kettle on.'

'She's been a good pal to me,' Mary said. 'Her and Sandra. I didnae take to her at first, you know. Janet, I mean. She looked that posh compared wi' the rest of us, me especially. Her clothes have aw got them designer labels. I told her she looked like the Queen. Same kind of build as well.'

'She's not a bit snobby, though,' Sandra said.

'Never was,' Mary agreed. 'Not a bit. No, it was just me getting the wrong end of the stick.'

Once Janet returned, they all relaxed as they supped at the mugs of hot, comforting liquid Janet had passed around. Eventually Sandra said, 'I was talking to Cheryl from upstairs.'

'Oh yes,' Janet passed around a plate of digestive biscuits. 'She's got a flat, hasn't she? In the West End? She seemed very happy.'

'Aye, her and Tommy,' Mary agreed. 'Nice lad.'

Sandra gave a big sigh. 'That's where I should be. Although having said that, after all that's happened, I think I'd be better to start a new life in some other district now.

Especially after all my in-laws said about me and with them being still there.'

'Something'll turn up, hen. I'm sure Betty's doing everything she can.'

'Cheryl said we must all go and visit her once she's settled in.'

Alice closed her eyes. 'The mere thought . . .'

'Listen, hen. It's high time you got a grip of yourself. You're getting really ridiculous now. You cannae shut yourself away for the rest of your life. An' we're no' going to let you. Are we, girls?'

'No.'

They all agreed and Rita added, 'We mustn't let the bastards win. Let's all start saving up to go out together for a really posh meal in a hotel in town. That'll give us something special to look forward to. Meantime, we should get a bit more fresh air and exercise by having walks through the park.'

'That's a good idea,' Janet said. 'We don't take advantage often enough of having such a beautiful park right on our doorstep. Even just now, it looks lovely.'

Alice's face had gone pale.

'I don't think I could – not after that last time . . . Mr Clarke seeing me . . .'

'That's ages ago now.' Rita rolled her eyes. 'And nothing's come of it. Anyway, even if he told your husband and even if your husband found you, what could he do? If you don't want to go back to him, you just refuse to go and if he bothers you, you phone the police.'

'Aye, hen. It's time you got a grip of yourself. OK?'

Alice nodded.

27

Mabel had to phone for the doctor. He gave her a ticking off for not having had the flu jab earlier. He also said that it was high time she was thinking of 'alternative accommodation', as he put it. She took that to mean an old-folks' home or a nursing home. Even the thought made her feel keenly apprehensive. There had been some horrific cases reported in the news recently about helpless old people being neglected and abused.

She tried to put on a brave face in front of the doctor. She even laughed.

'Oh, I'm not ready to give up the ghost just yet, Doctor. I enjoy my independence.'

The doctor shook his head. 'You're obviously not fit to do anything at the moment. I'll arrange for someone to call in and give you a hand until you're able to get up and about again. At the same time, I'll make some enquiries about alternative accommodation. The quicker the better. There's often a waiting list but a letter from me should help.'

She tried not to think about that and only be grateful for the help at present. She felt far from well, unable even to get up and make herself a cup of tea. As it turned out, the carer was very kind and attentive. She came in the morning to heelp her to get up, washed and dressed. And she popped in again in the evening to get her settled in bed. She liked to chat as well and Mabel began not only to look forward to her visits but also to dread when they would stop. It wasn't so much for any physical help, it would be the cheerful company she would miss. Any kind of company was a blessing she would have been grateful for. Loneliness had become unbearable. It took every remaining vestige of her will-power not to weep broken-heartedly when she had to say goodbye to the carer.

The house had never seemed so silent. She hobbled through to the kitchen to fill the kettle. Then, sitting nursing her cup of tea beside the electric fire, she became aware of the howling of the wind outside. She had heard it many times before. It was a common feature of high-rise living. Never before, however, had it sounded so ghostly and menacing. It increased her feeling of loneliness, of helplessness, of fear, a hundredfold.

Later, in the kitchen, she filled a basin with water in which to wash her supper dishes and, leaning against the sink, she watched the water slop backwards and forwards, backwards and forwards. This continuous swaying of the building was another feature of The Heights and other tower blocks. Water was never still or calm. In the sink, in the bath, in the lavatory pan, water moved with the movement of the building as it swayed in the wind. When her parents were alive, Mabel had seldom time during the day to notice the swaying, or the depressing sounds. She was too busy running about attending to all the needs of her mother and father. Then at night she usually fell into an exhausted sleep.

Now every dismal moan and howl echoed in her heart.

The only thing that kept her going was the thought of getting enough strength back in order to visit Bearsden. She clung to the vision of sitting at the window of the baker's café watching for her dearest John. She would know him when she saw him and just the sight of him would give her comfort and strength. She needed to be near him. She missed him so painfully. Perhaps he would come into the baker's – even sit in the café. Perhaps she would hear his voice again. A little spurt of excitement cheered her and made her feel that perhaps life would be worth living after all.

She could make it a regular jaunt. After all, as a pensioner, she had free travel on the buses and a cup of tea and perhaps a sandwich wouldn't cost too much. She could sit most of the day there. A cup of tea for elevenses. Then a cup of tea and a sandwich at lunchtime. It would be cheery there with all the customers coming in and out of the baker's for their purchases, as well as others stopping to enjoy a drink of something and a snack. The bakery counter was down one side and the café tables clustered down the other. Apart from the prospect of seeing John, it would be a cheerier way to pass the day than sitting alone in The Heights.

If she felt able, she might take a wee walk along Drymen Road and have a look at the other shops there. Her proposed visit to Bearsden filled her every waking hour now. All she had to do was regain enough strength to put her dreams into practice. The flu had drained away what little strength she'd normally had. But now, she told herself, she had something to live for, to look forward to. It would be even better than looking forward to John's daily phone calls.

The difficulty was she had run out of food in the house and so had nothing to eat to build up her strength. It was late afternoon and it was dark and wild-looking outside. Nevertheless, she got dressed, put on her coat and hat and forced herself out on to the landing. Once there, she felt quite faint with weakness. Determinedly she pressed for the lift. When it came, leaning heavily on her stick, she managed to enter it. The girl called Cheryl was the only other occupant.

'Hello, Miss Smith.'

Mabel smiled in response, then weakness overcame her

and the next thing she knew, she was on the floor of the lift and Cheryl was holding her.

'Oh, I'm sorry for being such a nuisance.' Mabel struggled to get up.

'Nothing to be sorry about.' Cheryl helped her to her feet. 'You're not a nuisance. But you don't look able to be out. I haven't seen you for a few days. Have you been ill?'

'Yes, a dose of flu. I'm all right now but I've run out of food and milk and I have to go out to the shops. I miss my cup of tea.'

'Och, you'll do no such thing. I'll take you back home and then I'll run along to the local shops for whatever you need.'

'How kind you are. Once I get a cup of tea and something to eat, I'll soon get my strength back.'

'OK. What floor are you on, again?'

'The twenty-fifth.'

'Right.' Cheryl pressed the button for the twenty-fifth floor and in a matter of seconds was helping Mabel out of the lift and across the landing. Mabel fumbled in her pocket for her key.

'Here, let me do it,' Cheryl plunged her hand in, came out with the key, opened the door and switched on all the lights.

'Come on now, settle yourself down by the fire and tell me everything you need.'

Tears blurred Mabel's eyes. What a kind girl Cheryl was.

'Oh, just the basic things, I think. Bread, margarine, milk.'

'I'll go and check.' Before Mabel could make any attempt to stop her, Cheryl had gone through to the kitchen. Embarrassed and ashamed, Mabel listened to fridge and cupboard doors opening and shutting. She knew only too well that all of them were completely empty.

When Cheryl came back, she said, 'What about your pension? Has anybody collected it for you?'

Mabel shook her head.

'Well, first of all, let's get organised with that so that I can collect it for you and then get all the groceries you need.'

Weak tears overflowed.

'You're so kind.'

'Don't be daft. I'm only sorry I won't be able to help you for long. I'm leaving. Did you know?'

Mabel nodded.

'But don't worry. I'll have a word with Mammy. I'm sure she'll keep an eye on you and give you a helping hand when you need it.'

And off she went, calling at the door, 'Won't be long.'

Mabel dozed off with relief and was awakened by Cheryl saying, 'Are you OK?'

'Oh!' Mabel jerked awake. 'I must have dozed off.'

'I got everything and that's your change on the table. I'll make you a cup of tea and something to eat before I leave.'

'Oh no, Cheryl. You've done enough already.'

'Just a wee sandwich, then. That won't take a minute.' And off she went to the kitchen. Oh, to have such youthful energy, Mabel thought. In a few minutes, Cheryl had returned with a couple of sandwiches and a piece of sponge cake on a plate.

'Just cheese and tomato. But it'll put some strength in you. I've got the kettle on. Just the tea to make and then I'll be off.'

Mabel bit gratefully into the sandwich. She hadn't realised until now how hungry she was. She was just beginning to enjoy the sandwich when she heard a cry of 'Oh, no!'

Cheryl came through and lifted some money from the table.

'Would you believe it, I've forgotten the tea. I'll just run back along for it. Won't be a minute.'

And she was gone before Mabel could utter a word of protest. Oh, how sorry she was that Cheryl was leaving – going away to the other side of the town, too. Just as she had made a friend, she was going to lose her. And such a good friend. But perhaps Cheryl's mother would prove to be a friend. Mabel couldn't remember ever seeing her. Or perhaps she had seen her but hadn't known who she was. There were so many occupants of so many flats in The Heights, it was easy to become confused, or to spend a lifetime not knowing anybody.

She finished her sandwiches and then enjoyed the cake. She thought the sweetness of the cake made her feel even better than the sandwiches. Now she was looking forward to a cup of tea. She relaxed back on to the cushions of the chair and gradually dozed off again.

It was the chiming of the clock that awakened her. She took off her glasses and rubbed her eyes. Then she sat for a few minutes, listening, wondering if Cheryl was back and in the kitchen. But there was only the moaning and howling of the wind. Mabel looked at the clock. She could hardly believe her eyes. Cheryl must have been away for over an hour.

'Cheryl,' she called out. No reply. 'Cheryl, are you in the kitchen?'

Still no reply.

Mabel grasped her stick, struggled to her feet and made her way through the hallway. The light was on in the kitchen but the kitchen was empty.

Perhaps Cheryl had to wait in a queue at the grocer's. But surely not for over an hour? Mabel slowly returned to her chair. She couldn't understand it. The grocer's couldn't be *that* busy. Perhaps they had run out of tea and Cheryl had gone down to Springburn to search for some. But for a grocer's to run out of tea! Tea of all things! In all her long life, Mabel had never heard of such a thing.

Another hour dragged past. Now she felt really worried. She developed a throbbing headache with worry. Something must have happened to Cheryl. Cheryl was so obviously a kind girl, she wouldn't have just left her like this when she said she would be back. Mabel felt distressed. She didn't know what to do.

Eventually she decided to go upstairs to Cheryl's house and ask Cheryl's mother if she knew what might have happened. Anyway, her mother ought to be told about how kind Cheryl had been and now how worried Mabel was about her.

Mabel had heard that Cheryl lived on the top floor and so, once out on the landing and then in the lift again, she pressed the button for number thirty. Once on the top floor, she hesitated for a minute or two, trying to remember Cheryl's second name. She dragged herself around to peer at all the name plates. She thought Patterson sounded familiar and so she pressed that button. A small, gently smiling lady opened the door.

'I'm Miss Smith from downstairs.'

'Oh, hello.' Puzzlement added a slight strained look to Mrs Patterson's face.

'I was wondering if you'd seen Cheryl recently.'

'She went out to meet her boyfriend.'

'When was that?'

'Why do you ask?'

Mabel shifted awkwardly on her stick and tried to lean against the door lintel for support.

'Come in and have a seat, Miss Smith. You don't look too well.'

Mabel followed Mrs Patterson into a surprisingly bare and shabby sitting room. Although when she thought of it, Mr Patterson was well known as an alcoholic and no doubt kept the family painfully short of money. They would not be able to afford many, if any, comforts. Not even a television, Mabel noticed.

'Now, what were you saying about Cheryl, Miss Smith?'

Mabel explained about how kind Cheryl had been and how she had even run back to the grocer's for the tea.'

'Yes, that's just like our Cheryl. An awful good girl. She's been so good and kind to me over the years. I'll miss her terribly when she moves over to the West End.'

'But, but . . . she didn't come back.'

'Didn't come back from where?'

'The grocer's. I fell asleep and when I woke up, I realised she'd been away over an hour – well over an hour.'

Mrs Patterson looked worried now but she said, 'Och well, she probably came back and, when she saw you asleep, she just left the tea in the kitchen. She wouldn't want to waken you, that's all.'

'No, I looked. She's never been back and I'm so worried.'

'Maybe she suddenly realised how late she was going to be to meet Tommy.' Mrs Patterson sounded faint, as if she was trying, but failing, to convince herself. 'And felt she had to rush to him in case he got worried.'

'Would he not have phoned?'

Mrs Patterson avoided Mabel's eyes.

'We haven't got a phone. We used to have but . . .'

'Oh dear. I hope she's all right.'

An urgent knocking at the door startled them both. Then the doorbell rang.

Mrs Patterson hurried to answer it. Then Mabel heard a man's voice.

'Is Cheryl here, Mrs Patterson? I waited for ages for her but she never turned up. Is she all right?'

28

'I've been here before,' Janet told the others. 'At a big dinner with my husband and some of his legal colleagues. It used to be called the Albany Hotel.'

They had all come dressed in their best but Janet, in her designer label lavender-coloured suit and matching hat tipped to one side at a fetching angle, looked, as Mary said, 'real posh'. They had booked a table for seven o'clock but they had come early so that they could relax in the bar for a 'wee refreshment' before going through to the dining room.

'Now remember what I told you,' Janet's voiced lowered towards Mary.

'Aye, aye, ginger beer for me. Nothing stronger. Don't worry.'

As they settled at a table in the long side area that led from the foyer, Alice said, 'We never used to go out much. Never at all, eventually. I was like a prisoner in my own house.'

'That was like me.' Sandra's eyes widened. 'It was absolutely terrible. I remember one time . . .'

Rita interrupted, 'For pity's sake, we're here to enjoy ourselves. I'll get the drinks.'

The bar was a recessed counter opposite the tables where the bar staff were busily serving customers. Rita ordered a drink for each of them and returned carrying a tray.

Janet tutted. 'You should have allowed the bar staff to bring it over.'

'I couldn't wait. I'm dying for a drink. It was good of Dorothy to volunteer to stay and see to my kids, wasn't it?'

'A wee gem,' Mary said. 'These lasses will have a place waitin' for them in heaven, so they will. Are you all right, hen?'

'How do you mean?' Rita knocked back her whisky.

'You're very tense-looking, Rita,' Janet said kindly. 'Just try to relax. As you said yourself, we're here to enjoy ourselves.'

Sandra rolled her eyes.

'I don't blame Rita. After all, her husband's a commercial traveller. He stays in hotels like this all the time. He could be in this one right now and come and drag her away.'

'Gee, thanks a bunch, Sandra.'

'Look, hen, even if he is here and even if he comes up tae you, we'll soon send him packin'. Won't we girls?'

'Yes, indeed,' Janet said. 'The same goes for all of us. We protect each other. That's what we've all agreed.'

After a few minutes, as they sipped their drinks, Rita burst out, 'I've a confession to make. I picked this hotel specially. It's the one he always stays at when he's in Glasgow.'

'Why on earth did ye do that, hen?'

'Well, I'm sick and tired of living in fear, cooped up in that flat. Oh, I know, I'm lucky to be there,' she added hastily, 'but I can't go on like this. I have to face up to him, once and for all, and I thought the best – the safest – way to do it was to have you lot here with me. Sorry, girls.'

'Don't worry, hen. He cannae take on all of us. He'll have me to reckon with, for a start.'

The others couldn't help smiling. Alice giggled at the vision of poor wee, one-armed Mary standing up to anybody, especially a man.

However, they enjoyed their drinks and then trooped through to the dining room without having seen anything of any belligerent man. It was a carvery meal. At the long counter, a chef was serving a hot dish of your choice, expertly cutting turkey and beef. A choice of vegetarian dishes was also on display, as well as separate platters of roast potatoes, sprouts and carrots. But first, at a central table, there were lots of tasty-looking starters and little dishes of sauces and chutney.

The girls helped themselves to rollmop herring, smoked salmon and salads before returning to their table.

'Isn't this great?' Alice enthusiastically munched into the food. 'I've never had a meal made for me like this for . . . oh, I can't remember when. I'm really enjoying it. Will there be a sweet as well, do you think?'

'Of course,' Janet assured her. 'But first there's the main course. What do you think you'll have for that? I'm going to have the turkey. But I remember the beef and Yorkshire puddings were excellent.'

In no time they were back at the chef's counter getting their plates full of food again and ordered coffee to be served with the sweet.

'Here, we should do this more often,' Sandra laughed. 'This is the life for me.'

Even Rita had begun to relax and laugh a little with the others. Every now and again, though, her eyes flicked anxiously towards the door.

Eventually, the meal over, Janet said, 'Let's go back to the bar and have one last drink before we get one of the staff to phone for a taxi.'

'Aye, right ye are. Can I no' even have a wee cider, Janet? Cider's no' alcoholic.'

'You know perfectly well it is, Mary.'

Mary sighed. 'There's no pullin' the wool over your eyes, is there, hen?'

'No, there is not.'

'OK. OK. Ginger beer again. Actually I'm gettin' to quite like the stuff.'

'Good!' With dignity, Janet led the others from the dining room through to the bar area. There they became not only relaxed but giggly. They would have been quite content to sit there all night but, as Janet said, they couldn't do that. They'd already had one of the staff phone for a taxi and it was time to go and get their coats from the cloakroom at the foyer.

Happily, dreamily, waiting in the foyer, they were suddenly shattered by a man's voice calling out, 'Rita!'

'Christ, it's him,' Rita said.

A tall, slim man was striding towards them.

'Rita, darling. I've been so worried about you. Thank God I've found you.'

'Get your hands off me.' Rita shrank back.

'Come on, darling. I'll cancel my calls in Glasgow and we'll drive back home together to Aberdeen right now.'

Everyone closed around Rita and wee Mary said, 'She's no' goin' anywhere wi' you, so push off, mister.'

'She's my wife. Come on, Rita.'

Suddenly Rita came aggressively to life.

'Get your hands off me, you dirty pervert. I'm going nowhere with you. And if you don't get out of my way, I'll shout out right here and now exactly why I'm divorcing you. I'll let everyone know just what a dirty, perverted bastard you are. And if you ever come near me again, I'll do the same. No matter where it is.'

Janet took one of Rita's arms and Sandra linked Rita's other arm into hers and said, 'Come on, Rita. The taxi'll be outside by now. Let's go home.'

'Right. And you,' Rita shouted, 'you two-faced bastard, will be hearing from not only my lawyer but the police.'

The man paled and drew away. Without another word, he went over to the reception desk and, with his back to them, placed his briefcase on the counter and signed into the hotel.

Outside in the wet darkness, Rita said, 'Thank God!'

'Good for you,' Sandra said. 'You were great, Rita. Just great.'

'Aye, you fairly put his gas in a peep, hen.'

Once in the taxi and, after taking a fit of the giggles, helped no doubt by the drink they'd consumed and their relief at defeating Rita's husband, they burst into song.

They were still giggling and singing – albeit comparatively quietly – when they arrived at the safe house.

'My word, you've obviously had a good time,' Dorothy said. 'By the way, the children are all tucked up and sound asleep so don't go waking them up.'

Rita put her finger to her lips.

'Sh. Sh!'

Her eyes, normally dark with fear and suffering, had an unusual sparkle about them. 'I'd better get to my bed. See you in the morning, girls.' Just before she reached the door, she turned and said, 'And thanks.'

'You're welcome, hen.'

Rita gave them a wave before disappearing and Janet said, 'She'll probably be all right now.'

Alice sighed. 'I wish I had her nerve.'

'You'll be fine. We all will eventually.'

'Aye, so Betty keeps tellin' us.'

'At least, like Rita, I'm going to be legally free of my husband. I've got plenty of proof of his cruelty, what with his last assault not only causing me to lose my baby but . . .' She swallowed, then continued with difficulty. 'Because of him, I can't ever again . . .' She closed her eyes. 'Sorry.'

'Aye, well, it's him that should be made to feel sorry, hen.'

'I'll feel better once the divorce goes through. And I think I'll take a leaf out of Rita's book and threaten him with the police and even better, let everyone know – all his neighbours and friends and work mates – what he did to me, shout it from the rooftops. When I think of it, that's the very worst that could happen as far as he's concerned.' She laughed. 'Gosh, yes. I can imagine his face if I threatened that. He's a civil servant, of all things.'

'Aye but no' very civil to you, eh?'

'Do you know, I suddenly feel so much better. I think I'll even be able to sleep tonight without one of my sleeping tablets.'

'It's the drink, hen. Nothin' to beat it.'

'Talking of sleeping,' Janet yawned, 'I think it's time we were all in bed and enjoying a good night's sleep after all the merriment, not to mention the excitement with Rita.'

'Aye, an' the drink.'

'Will you stop talking about drink, Mary?'

'Ah never touched a drop, hen. Honestly.'

'I know but you must learn to banish all thoughts of it from your mind.'

'Aye, OK, OK. Anything you say.'

'I'm so glad about Rita,' Alice said.

'Aye, I bet she'll be able to get up enough nerve now to have a go in a house on her own. She was offered one, remember, but at the time was too frightened to leave here.'

'Yes,' Janet said thoughtfully. 'One does get very dependent on Betty and Dorothy. But at least I've spoken to my solicitor and started divorce proceedings now.'

'Ah don't know about Betty and Dorothy, hen, but I'm dependent on you. You and Sandra.'

Sandra put her arm around Mary's shoulders. 'You'd manage great on your own. You've a very independent spirit, Mary. You've always had a wonderful spirit.'

'For pity's sake, will ye stop mentioning that word.'

They all laughed then.

'Seriously though, I always had a spunky nature but nowadays . . . I mean, look at me wi' Chrissie Cumberland. If it hadnae been for you two . . . No, I'm nae use without ma pals and I know it.'

Janet hugged her then. But both she and Sandra felt worried.

29

'A cup of tea, please.' Mabel smiled at the woman behind the counter.

'Milk and sugar's on the table. Hang on, I'll come round and carry the cup over for you.'

'Thank you, you're very kind. I'd like to sit at the window, if you don't mind.'

Mabel's stick clicked on the floor as she followed the assistant along to a table from which she could watch not only all the passers-by in Drymen Road but also any customers at the bakery counter. With a sigh of relief and another smile at the assistant, she propped her stick against one of the chairs and relaxed back as comfortably as she could. Then she took a grateful sip of the tea.

This cup of tea would have to last her a long time. She planned to have another cup and perhaps a sandwich and that would serve as lunch. That way she could sit for an extra hour or two.

It was difficult to relax and get back to her feelings of happy anticipation of this visit to Bearsden. She was still upset and worried about Cheryl.

Mrs Patterson had taken her back downstairs after Tommy had arrived.

'Now, don't you worry, Miss Smith,' Mrs Patterson told

her. 'We'll find Cheryl all right. There's bound to be some perfectly simple explanation. Nothing for you to get so upset about.'

In actual fact, it was Mrs Patterson who looked so upset. Even her voice was shaking.

Mabel said, 'You'll let me know if anything's happened to Cheryl?'

'Of course.'

Mrs Patterson had not let her know anything. Mabel took it to mean that, thankfully, no accident or anything bad had happened to Cheryl. Perhaps Cheryl might pop in to see her this evening after she finished work. If she'd time, of course. Cheryl would be very busy getting ready for her move to Byres Road and also looking for a job in the West End. It had been so kind of her in those circumstances to take time to help.

'It's not fair of me to expect the girl to get back to me,' Mabel thought. 'She's got enough on her mind just now without bothering about my shopping.'

She took another sip of her tea and peered out of the window. It was a busy main road and a steady stream of people kept passing to and fro. Sometimes a woman would stop to speak to another. Sometimes people would come into the shop. Mabel turned her attention towards the bakery counter. One of the customers was a man. It wasn't John. This man was short and stockily built and he was wearing filthy boots, a dirty pair of denims and a huge, hooded, yellow waterproof jacket. Mabel guessed he was one of the workmen digging up the roads. John was very tall and slim and had described himself as being 'a respectable businessman'.

Some people, mostly women, came in and collected tea, coffee or soft drinks at the café extension of the bakery counter. Then they settled down at one of the tables to enjoy a chat.

After a time, a very long time it seemed, Mabel's chair had become so hard and uncomfortable that she decided to get up and take a short walk along Drymen Road to stretch her legs. She could take it slowly. There was no hurry. She had all day. Next to Auld's Bakery and Coffee Shop, as she discovered it was called, there was an optometrist's. Then the Royal Bank of Scotland, then a barber's shop. Mabel remembered when barbers always had red and white poles sticking out above them. You didn't often see that nowadays. Long ago, barbers used to act as surgeons and the colours of the pole represented blood and bandages. Next to the barber's, there was a clothes shop called 'Classic Contour'. It had a sale on and there were very nice garments displayed in the window that had prices considerably reduced. All too expensive for her to think about, of course. She sighed to herself and moved on. A sportswear shop stretched around the corner on to the New Kirk Road. After resting for another minute or two, she crossed the road to where there was a paper shop at the opposite corner. She passed another bank, a restaurant called, oddly, 55 BC, and a card and fancy goods shop. She stopped to peer into a charity shop. By that time, she was too tired to go any further and so she turned back towards Auld's Bakery and Coffee Shop.

She was glad to get a seat again and to be served with another cup of hot tea. This time she treated herself to a sandwich. Later on, she might even have one of their delicious-looking scones. She used to be good at baking scones. She used to bake a good ginger cake as well. Her mother and father both enjoyed her ginger cakes. A faint mist of bitterness came back to haunt her when she thought of all she had done for her parents – devoted every minute of every day of her life to them. And oh, how they had taken her life for granted.

But what was the use of allowing them to spoil any small chance of happiness she had now? She banished them from her mind. She was happy at the moment – or as happy as she could be in the circumstances. The sandwich was tasty, the tea comforting and reviving, the surroundings cheerful and companionable. Most important of all, she was in Bearsden, near to John. Her heart warmed at the thought.

Her tea was almost finished. She had eaten every last crumb of her sandwich when she actually saw him. She saw John. She recognised him from his description right away. He was very tall and thin with a long-nosed, gaunt face and black hair that hung down over one side of his face. He had a slight stoop as if purposely trying to disguise his height.

Her heart quickened so much that she thought she was going to faint. He was standing in the queue at the bakery counter. She couldn't help feeling a pang of disappointment. Pity too. He was not an attractive man. He'd said that himself, of course. She realised now that she hadn't believed him at the time. Now, she even experienced a feeling of repulsion. She immediately quelled it. Poor man. She of all people should be able to sympathise with him. Wasn't she ugly too? Always had been.

'Two cheese rolls, please,' he asked the assistant.

It was him all right. She recognised his voice.

Her heart went out to him as it had done so many times when they had been speaking on the phone. He was a lonely man, as she was a lonely woman. Here he was buying his meagre lunch to eat on his own, as she was eating on her own. All her gratitude for being here, for being near him, returned. She could have wept with it. Her reason for living returned. There were no longer his phone calls to look forward to but this was even better. For as long as she was able, she would come here every day and be near to John.

She watched him leave the shop and turn right along Drymen Road. She strained closer to the window but a group of women standing gossiping outside blocked her view.

She relaxed back in her chair again. She had seen John. Her poor, dear John who'd had to phone a stranger to find even an illusion of love. She had been close to him, first on the phone and now here, in the flesh. He had been only a few feet away from her. Next time, she'd try to be ready to follow him out of the shop and hopefully discover where his business was and what kind of business he owned. Next time, as soon as he entered the bakery, she would struggle up, leave the shop before he was served and then pretend to look in another shop window while she waited for him to reappear from the bakery.

The more she knew about him, the closer to him she'd feel. And the happier. She looked forward to many return visits. She sat for a long time after seeing him, savouring her thoughts and her memories of their many phone conversations. She was so glad she had now seen him in the flesh. Sometimes she used to feel that it was all a dream. That somehow John wasn't real. Now she knew beyond all doubt that he did exist in reality. It was exciting to the point of being overwhelming. She had to sit for quite a time, even to have another cup of tea, before she felt fit enough to struggle to her feet and leave the shop. Unfortunately, she just missed a bus. She saw it coming but she was unable to hurry in order to catch it. As a result, she had ages to wait for the next one. Or so it seemed. Then of course she had to catch another bus from town to take her back to The Heights.

It seemed a miracle that she managed to arrive back in her flat without collapsing with fatigue. Through in the sitting room, she relaxed back in her easy chair and gave a sigh of relief. Tonight she would have an early night. As it was, she dozed off in the chair before she even had taken her coat and hat off.

She awakened with a start and it took a few seconds before she realised that the phone was ringing. It lay on a little table at her elbow. She picked it up, thinking it would be John. But, as she became properly awake, she realised it couldn't be.

'Hello?'

'It's Mrs Patterson. Thank goodness I've got you at last. We've never been off Tommy's mobile all day, phoning and phoning you.'

'Oh, I'm sorry. I had to go out. I'm not long back.' Then a thought struck her. Her voice turned anxious. She had become aware of the distress in Mrs Patterson's voice. 'Has something happened to Cheryl?'

'That's what the police want to ask you about.'

'What?'

'You were the last one to see her. The police want to question you. They've been trying to contact you all day as well.'

30

'Now I don't want to hear any "I told you so" from you.' Betty fixed Rita with an unusually stern eye. 'Especially to Kate. She's in pain, physically and mentally, and doesn't need you to be humiliating her and making her feel worse.'

'OK. OK.'

'Promise?'

Rita raised her hands. 'I promise.'

'She's having a cup of tea with Dorothy in the office just now. I'll bring her through in a couple of minutes. She's got fractured ribs so don't go hugging her either.'

'Don't worry,' Alice said. 'She'll be fine with us, won't she, Rita?'

'Yes, of course.'

But after Betty strode away, Rita said to Alice, 'A man of honour, she said. Just because he's a judge.'

'Rita, you promised.'

'I'm only saying to you. I'll not say anything to the poor cow. She must be feeling terrible.'

Kate Smythe-Bellingham looked terrible as well. Her face was grey and there were dark shadows under her tragic, staring eyes.

'You're all right now,' Rita said. 'You're safe.'

Betty was carrying Kate's suitcase. 'I'll put this through in your room, Kate, and I'll pop back later on to make sure you've settled in. All right?'

Kate nodded. Then she sank gingerly into one of the cushioned chairs beside the fire.

'Do you want another cup of tea?' Alice asked.

'No, thanks. You must think I'm very stupid.'

Rita lit a cigarette. 'No, no. It happens all the time. We all love the bastards at first and can't believe what they're really like. We all trust them at first.'

'I won't make that mistake again. I'm so glad I managed to get away. He nearly killed me.'

'Well, as I say, you're safe now.'

'You missed a great night out.' Alice's young face lit up, remembering. 'We went to the Holiday Inn for a meal and a few drinks. Then just as we were coming away, who did we bump into in the foyer but Rita's husband. She gave him a right showing up. It would have done your heart good to hear her.' She laughed. 'I bet he won't try anything on her again. You should have seen his face.'

'Good for you, Rita.' Kate attempted a smile. 'I admire your courage.'

'Och, I don't think I could have managed it if all the others hadn't been there. It was a great night, right enough.'

'How is wee Mary?'

'She's fine. Talk about courage? She's the one with the courage.'

'And Janet and Sandra?'

'Just the same. Janet's still the perfect lady and Sandra's still a drama queen.'

Kate smiled.

'Once I feel a bit stronger, I'll go and see them.'

'Don't worry.' Alice jumped up eagerly. 'I'll tell them you're here and they'll come to see you.'

In a few minutes, Alice was back with Janet, Sandra and wee Mary in tow. Sandra rushed over to hug Kate but Alice's shout stopped her just in time.

'Kate's ribs are fractured.'

'Oh, how awful. Oh Kate, I'm so sorry. Are you all right?'

Kate sighed. 'Well, I'm all right now, thank goodness.' She looked around the room. 'In a way, it's so strange to see this place again. I mean, it's so different from anywhere else, isn't it? All the lilac and green.'

'The suffragette colours,' Rita told her. 'They fought for their freedom and their rights and now we're fighting for ours.'

Kate sighed.

'I'm afraid I'm not much use as a fighter. I give up too easily.'

'You'll learn. You won't go back to him again, will you? You won't believe all that about him being a man of honour and being sorry, will you?'

'I sincerely hope not. He was worse. He was furious at me.'

'Oh yes, because other people know about him now. All the Women's Help people, not to mention all of us.'

Sandra's eyes widened dramatically.

'You didn't tell them this address, did you? When my husband found out this address, he came . . .'

'Yes, all right, Sandra,' Janet interrupted. 'We all know about that. We don't want to be reminded.'

'No, I didn't tell him. I pretended I didn't know where the Women's Help people had taken me. Then today, while he was in court, I phoned Betty on my mobile. I didn't even use the house phone in case he might trace the call.'

'Good for you,' Rita said. 'See, you are learning.'

'He wouldn't have come near here anyway. Not with him being a judge,' Alice said. 'Betty says men like that never want anybody to know that they're abusers.'

'Your husband was different, Sandra,' Janet got in quickly before Sandra could open her mouth. 'And he was mad with drugs. Or whatever the expression is. And your sister told him where you were – she admitted it to you.'

'I know. I thought I'd never forgive her for that but she's been inundating me with letters and phone calls ever since, telling me how sorry she is. She's even pleading with me to go through to Edinburgh to stay with her. The last time I told her I might think about it – at least until I get some place of my own.'

'That sounds like a good idea,' Janet said. 'I hope we'll keep in touch, though.'

'Of course. I'd come through for the get-together every second Friday.'

'That would be great, hen. Janet and me'll miss you but it wouldn't be so bad if we could keep in touch like that and keep up with all the news.'

'Talking about news . . .' Alice said. 'Have any of you spoken to Monty today?'

'No, we haven't been out for a few days.'

'Well, he was telling me that the police have been in the building.'

Wee Mary said, 'Och, that's nothing new, hen. Them young folk are always doing something to make Monty send for the local bobbies. Kicking balls against the door. Doing their graffiti – all sorts of things.'

'No, this was about Cheryl.'

'Something to do with Tommy again?'

'No, it was Tommy who reported it, apparently.'

'Reported what?'

'She's gone missing.'

'Cheryl?'

'Yes. They've been looking for Miss Smith as well.'

'Miss Smith?' Janet gasped in astonishment. 'That old lady from upstairs?'

'Monty says she must have had something to do with it.'

'Don't be daft,' Mary said. 'The poor old soul's half blind and can hardly walk.'

'Well, Monty says the police want to talk to her.'

'Monty's a right old gossip, hen.'

'Why would he say such a thing if it wasn't true? He stopped me especially to tell me.'

'Och, you know fine that he does that to everybody. It's how he spends half his day.'

Nevertheless, Alice wasn't convinced by what Janet and wee Mary were saying.

'Well, I believe him. There's something happened to Cheryl. What do you bet?'

Janet was beginning to look unsure. 'I hope not. It's enough to make us all feel nervous.'

'Apparently she was supposed to meet Tommy and she never turned up. He waited for ages. Then he came to The Heights to see if she was at her mother's but she'd left to meet him, her mother said.'

'But what could Miss Smith have to do with it?'

'Tommy says she went for some messages for her and that was the last time she was seen.'

'Well, if that's true,' Janet said, 'they'll want to talk to Miss Smith about the time she last saw Cheryl, things like that.'

'Monty said they couldn't find Miss Smith the first time they came. He doesn't know if they came back and had any better luck. He was off duty.'

'She was probably away for the day somewhere.'

Alice shook her head. 'I can't see her going far or for very long. I don't really know the woman, of course. I'm just going by the look of her. She can barely hobble along on that stick.'

Suddenly they were startled by a ring on the doorbell and Betty's voice shouting through the letter box, 'It's only me.'

Janet went to let her in and when her tall, solid figure appeared in the sitting room, she greeted everybody with 'Hello folks. Everything OK?'

'Yes . . .' Janet hesitated. 'Except we're worried about what's happened to Cheryl from upstairs. Is it true what Monty's been saying? Is she missing?'

'Yes, that's what I'm in about. The police have been knocking on every door from the top flat downwards. They'll be at us soon. They just want to know when everybody last saw Cheryl or talked to her and how she seemed. Did she look or sound worried or anything? All that sort of stuff. I thought I'd better warn you – in case you got a fright when the police came to the door.'

'Thank you, Betty. That was good of you.'

'Poor Cheryl.' Sandra gazed dramatically up through her fringe. 'She's probably been murdered.'

Alice groaned. 'Are you purposely trying to frighten me? You know how nervous I can be.'

'Well, what else could have happened? Disappearing like that and her so much in love with Tommy and just about to start a new life with him. She wouldn't just disappear off her own bat.'

'She could have been involved in an accident,' Betty said firmly, 'and be lying in hospital somewhere. It's no help speculating and thinking the worst. Just answer any questions the police ask – *truthfully*. Just what you *know*.' She fixed Sandra with a warning look. 'Not what you imagine.'

'God!' Rita inhaled deeply at her cigarette. 'What a terrible worry for her mother. The bloody father's probably too drunk to care.'

'And Tommy,' Alice said. 'He'll be worried sick as well.'

'Aye. He seems such a nice fella. A right worry, so it is.'

Sandra rolled her eyes. 'And him barely recovered from nearly being burned to death.'

'Well,' Betty said, 'we'll just have to hope everything works out all right. Meantime, try not to worry.'

Just then, there was a loud knocking and Betty went to answer it. She came back followed by two very large policemen.

All the women fell silent. Even Sandra.

31

It had been a nuisance having to run back out for the tea after she'd forgotten it the first time. It was a wild night and one of the street lamps wasn't working. It made the dark night even darker.

Probably one of the local youths had flung a brick or something at the lamp. They were always doing something. Apart from anything else, they spoiled the look of the whole place with graffiti. And it was a disgrace the way they kept dropping litter about.

Cheryl was worried about being late for Tommy. However, once she had told him about Miss Smith, he'd understand. Tommy was kind and good-hearted. He'd want to help the poor old thing as well. Anyway, she wouldn't be that late if she ran both ways and didn't go back into Miss Smith's, just gave her the tea at her door. She could apologise for not having enough time to make a pot of tea but would promise to look in on her again the first chance she got.

The grocer's wasn't too busy and she was in and out in no time. Clutching at the plastic bag with the tea inside, she began running up the dark road as fast as she could. After a couple of minutes, she imagined she heard running footsteps behind her but didn't take time to turn and look.

Then suddenly she felt a terrible pain in the back of her head. She knew she had been struck on the head with something but, before she was able to form another thought, her legs buckled and she slid into unconsciousness.

She awoke slowly to the sounds of her own muffled groaning. Her heart leapt with panic as she began to realise that there was a blindfold round her eyes, something tied over her mouth and her hands and feet were bound. Her surroundings felt icy cold. Damp too. A sickening smell filled her nostrils. She couldn't understand what was happening. It was like something out of a horror film. Who in real life would want to do this to her? She had no enemies that she knew of. It was totally beyond understanding.

People didn't get kidnapped in Springburn or Balornock.

Then, terrifyingly, she heard a man's voice. He was saying, 'I didn't want it to be this way, Angela. I pleaded with you. Over and over again, I gave you the chance to meet me and begin a proper relationship. A normal relationship.' His voice trembled. 'You said you loved me. I believed you. Yet all the time, you were seeing another man. I've watched you with him. I know all about him. Why did you do it, Angela? It's not even as if he was anything special. Anything better than me. I'm a successful businessman. I could have given you a good life and a lovely home. What could he give you?'

Cheryl twisted her head from side to side. She knew now what must have happened. It was mistaken identity. This man, whoever he was, had mistaken her for somebody else. Somebody called Angela. Yet how could that have happened? Had she a double, or what?

'All right,' he was saying. 'I'll take the gag off and give you a drink from this bottle of water. But there's no use trying to make any noise. No one could possibly hear you, believe me.'

She felt his fingers fumble at the back of her head. The gag came away from her mouth.

'You've made a terrible mistake.' Desperate words rushed out. 'My name's not Angela. I'm Cheryl Patterson from The

Heights. I don't know any Angela. I've never heard of anybody called Angela.'

There was an uneasy silence.

'I swear as God's my witness, I don't know anybody called Angela. I'm Cheryl Patterson and I live with my mammy and daddy on the thirtieth floor of The Heights. Ask anybody. Phone anybody. Check any way you like.'

She could hear the man's heavy breathing. She began to sob.

'Please let me go back to my mammy. She'll be worried sick about me.'

She became aware of movement. Then footsteps.

'Please let me go,' she cried out. 'Please don't leave me here.'

But she knew instinctively that he'd gone.

★★★★★

Ingram thought he was going mad. He had meant to try yet again to reason with Angela, to persuade her to see sense, to somehow make her want to give him a chance. She would surely realise that to go to such extreme measures to get together with her proved that he genuinely loved her and had a desperate need to be with her.

He would apologise for hurting her but, he would explain, she gave him no choice and he would make up for it, if she just gave him the chance. For the rest of his life, he would be good to her, never lift a finger to hurt her again. He would do anything and everything he could to make up for it. He would swear it.

If they could just talk again as they had done so often in the past, they would be able to work something out, he was sure.

That's how he had persuaded himself. That's why he had loosened the gag. The woman's voice still reverberated in his brain. Not the lovely gentle lilting Highland voice of Angela but a loud, coarse, common Glasgow voice.

The voice confused and shocked him. No way could that voice belong to Angela. He loped away through the car park, along New Kirk Road, round on to Drymen Road and up the stairs to his flat. His brain was still reeling. He collapsed into a chair and with shaking fingers, managed to light a cigarette. He inhaled deeply. He downed a stiff whisky. Nothing helped.

How could this be? The description of the girl exactly matched in every way what Angela had told him – even every piece of clothing matched. Every time he saw her, and he'd seen her quite a few times now, everything matched exactly. Her hair, her features, her figure, her clothes, everything. Exactly. Yet it was not her. He thought for a long time. He lit another cigarette. He had another whisky. Gradually, an explanation came to him. Angela must have been describing someone else. She had done it purposely to fool him.

Hatred and rage were so strong, it set his mind on fire. That was it. He'd kill the cruel, devious bitch. He'd find her and kill her. No kidnapping. No talking. He'd just quietly, swiftly, cut her throat.

Then he remembered the girl in the bomb shelter and felt confused again. And frightened. He wished her no harm. Nothing was her fault. But what could he do? He daren't be seen by her. If he let her go and she saw him, she would report him and his description to the police. That way, Angela would win again.

Yet if he just left her there, she could die. He had been telling her the truth when he said if she screamed, nobody would hear her. There was the odd chance of children wandering along near there during the summer holidays. He couldn't imagine them going along there in the dark, especially venturing into the damp, stinking depths of the air-raid shelter.

He tried to think of all possibilities of releasing the girl. Could he undo the rope around her wrists and then make a run for it in the hope that he'd be well out of sight before she undid the blindfold and the rope around her ankles? That would be taking a terrible risk. He might make it to the car park. But what about the lights there and in all the surrounding streets? He was so tall he would stick up like a running telegraph pole no matter what way he took. He cursed his height. He cursed Angela for the terrible predicament she'd got him into. Oh, he'd kill her all right.

At least he knew where she lived. She was obviously from The Heights. She must be able to see this other girl regularly in order to describe her so often and in such detail.

What an evil bitch she was, putting another girl at risk like that. An innocent girl. He felt physically sick with hatred. No more talking. No more second chances. No more love. It had all been an illusion.

The cruel, sadistic bitch. How she'd made him suffer. Never in his wildest dreams had he ever imagined anybody being so devious and cruel. He thought about the other girl again. Poor cow. It was terrible. He had to think of something. Some way to free her. Save her. But he couldn't come up with any ideas at all. As each tortuous minute passed, rage and hatred burned deeper into his brain until all he could see in his mind's eye was his father's open razor slicing across Angela's throat.

*****

It was the talk of The Heights. What on earth could have happened to Cheryl? No way could she have disappeared of her own volition. Not when she was to meet Tommy and they were about to move in together into a lovely flat in the West End. Cheryl had been so happy she'd told everyone about it.

'Something terrible must have happened,' Sandra insisted. 'She's been kidnapped and murdered. I bet you anything.'

'But why?' Janet asked. 'Who would want to do that to Cheryl, of all people? Such a nice, kind girl.'

'Her mammy's in a terrible state and no wonder,' Mary said. 'And so is Tommy.'

'Yes,' Kate joined in. 'Monty says poor Tommy is nearly demented. He's searching everywhere. He's been through every inch of the park already.'

'Even that drunken bum of a father of hers is helping with the search,' Rita said. 'And according to what I've heard, he's even gone off the drink.'

Kate shook her head. 'I'm sorry for Miss Smith as well. She feels guilty because Cheryl had gone out for her messages but, as Betty said, it wasn't Miss Smith's fault. Cheryl was going out anyway.'

Mary sighed. 'I'd better make a move. Betty wants a word with me in the office. I hope it's no' to give me a tellin' off about something I've done wrong.'

'Don't be daft, Mary,' Sandra said. 'You've done nothing wrong. We'll all stick up for you, don't worry.'

'Thanks, hen.'

She struggled up with the help of her one arm pushing against the arm of the chair. 'I'll let you know when I come back in.'

After she left, Rita asked, 'She hasn't been drinking again, has she?'

Janet gave her a stern, disapproving look.

'Certainly not. She's been as good as gold. Hasn't she, Sandra?'

'Yes, definitely. I'll miss her . . . and all of you, when I go to Edinburgh. Here, you'll let me know if anything's found out about Cheryl, won't you?'

'Yes, of course. When is it you said your sister's coming for you?'

'The end of the week. In just a couple of days. My brother-in-law is bringing her through in their car. I'm quite looking forward to it now. Except, as I say, I'll miss you all.'

'Oh well, you'll come occasionally to the get-togethers, no doubt.'

'Not occasionally, Janet. I'll come to every one.'

'Now, now, you're exaggerating again, Sandra. Once you get a job in Edinburgh, you'll not be able to come through here every time.'

'Yes, I will. If the get-togethers are held in the evening and I work during the day, there'll be no problem.'

Just then, wee Mary re-entered the room.

'Well?' Sandra asked.

Instead of answering, Mary said, 'You next, Rita.'

'Me?' Rita looked indignant. 'I've done nothing bloody wrong.'

'Nobody's said you have, hen. Away you go through.'

Rita had barely disappeared when Sandra impatiently repeated, 'Well?'

Mary sighed. 'You'll never guess.'

'For goodness' sake, Mary. Tell us.'

'Houses have come up and I've been offered one.'

'Great! Great! That's really exciting, Mary. But why the long face?'

After a minute, Mary said, 'You're aw right, hen. You're goin' to live with your sister. I don't fancy stayin' anywhere by masel' now. I'm that used to my pal Janet, here. Naw, I cannae leave Janet.' She turned a pleading face to Janet. 'You'd miss me, hen, sure you would.'

'Of course I would, Mary. Where is the house?'

'Over in the south side. Betty says it's a flat in a nice red sandstone building and it's in a very nice street. Fancy, near another park, she says. Queen's Park.'

'Oh yes, that's a very nice respectable area.'

'Ah don't care what it's like. I don't care if it's Buckingham Palace. I'm no' leavin' you, hen.'

They all laughed at the ridiculous vision of wee Mary in Buckingham Palace.

'Ah'm glad you all think it's so funny,' Mary said, not looking glad at all.

'Mary,' Janet said. 'There might be a solution to this. Just give me a little time to think about it.'

32

It was a terrible nuisance Mrs Patterson not having a phone, although she said that she'd ordered one now. Tommy had told her that, in the circumstances, it was absolutely vital.

She told Mabel, 'I know that myself of course. What if Cheryl needed to get in touch with us by phone? I don't care what it costs now. Even if I've to work my fingers to the bone to pay for it.'

Poor Mrs Patterson, Mabel thought. She was in a state of near-collapse. Mr Patterson was having to stay off work to look after her. He was in a state as well. Anyway, the phone had not been installed yet and so Mabel had to go up in the lift to the thirtieth floor to talk to Mrs Patterson. She heard Mrs Patterson's feet running along the lobby in her haste to answer the bell.

'Oh!' The eager, hopeful look in her face immediately collapsed at the sight of Mabel. 'It's you, Miss Smith. Come in.'

'No, thank you all the same, but I wanted to let you know – in case I'm needed to answer any more questions or anything – that I'm away to visit a friend in Bearsden. I won't stay too long.'

'It's all right. I'm sure you won't be needed again, Miss Smith. You've already told us and the police everything you know.'

'Well, if you think so . . .'

'Yes, I'm absolutely sure. Please don't worry.'

The door shut and Mrs Patterson's feet, dragging this time, could be heard returning back along the lobby. Mabel went into the lift and took it down to the ground floor. She badly needed to get away from The Heights and all the worrying buzz of talk about Cheryl and what could have happened to her. Mabel felt she had to do something to distract herself, take her mind off the awful business. She would go and sit in Auld's Bakery and Coffee Shop and feel the comfort of being near to John. Perhaps John came into the shop every day to buy something for his lunch. She planned to go every day. One day he might decide to eat in the coffee shop. If the place was busy, he might even sit at the same table as her. Her pulse throbbed with excitement at the mere idea.

It was raining outside and she was finding it increasingly difficult, almost impossible, to keep her balance with the strength of the gale-force winds. If it hadn't been for the steadying help of her stick, she would definitely have been blown over. Indeed, as she was crossing the road, she staggered alarmingly and was only saved by a young woman rushing to grab her and help her to reach the bus stop.

Young people weren't all bad. After having got to know Cheryl and Tommy, she had no longer any doubt about that. This young woman (she had a metal bead or some such awful thing in her nose) even helped her on to the bus.

'Thank you, dear. You're very kind.'

'Cheers!' the girl said. She appeared to be chewing gum or something. Oh well, Mabel thought, what was the harm in that? She dozed off in the bus. She hadn't been sleeping well recently, what with all the anxiety and uncertainty about Cheryl. The building seemed weighted down with worry. Maybe it was her imagination but that's how it felt. She was really glad to get away from the place, even for just a few hours.

The bus driver had to waken her up at the bus station. He helped her off the bus.

'OK, hen?'

'Yes, thank you for your help. You're very kind.'

'All part of the job, darlin'. Have a nice day.'

Yes, she *would* have a nice day. A lovely day, if she saw John again. His too-tall, too-thin figure. His poor, unhandsome face. They had so much in common. She was not tall like him, of course. But her face was unattractive indeed. She and John were both lonely souls. They both needed to love and be loved.

When she eventually got off the Bearsden bus at the church, she waited patiently for an opportunity to cross the road safely. Slowly she hobbled past the barber's shop, the blue frontage of the Royal Bank and the optometrist's. Thankfully, she reached the coffee shop and lowered herself on to a chair at the window. The girl at the coffee counter who had served her previously called to her, 'It's all right. I'll bring it over. Tea, wasn't it?'

Mabel nodded. She was quite out of breath with her exertion.

The girl came over with a pot of tea, a pot of water and a cup and saucer. Mabel fumbled in her purse.

'How kind of you.' She was so lucky. People were proving to be really good to her.

'No bother. Enjoy your tea.'

'Thank you.'

She did enjoy it. And fancy getting a jug of hot water as well. Now she could have several cups if she wanted to. And she actually preferred weak tea.

Apart from waiting for John, it was quite a pleasant way to pass the time, watching the passers-by in the street outside. It was interesting as well to study the variety of people coming into the shop to buy bread or rolls or cakes or scones or pies or sausage rolls at the bakery counter. Then of course there were the people who filled the tables to enjoy a cup of tea or coffee or a chat with friends. The people sitting at the tables were mostly women. There were only a few men, retired probably and just passing the time, like her.

Her spirits rose. There, at last, was John. Her first and only love. Then, suddenly, she felt worried. His face looked so pale and drawn. Far more so than when she'd last seen him. Was he unwell? Or was he suffering so much because of her? She felt pain at the thought of the pain she had caused him. He could not understand. He would feel hurt and betrayed. She felt regret at ever having started the phone calls. She should never have contacted the agency in the first place. It had been a selfish and wicked thing to do. She ought to have known that no good would come of it.

She had an overwhelming desire to go over to the counter and stand beside him in the hope that somehow her desperate wish to comfort him would radiate from her to him and he would somehow be comforted. She could stand near to him, perhaps, with her arm actually touching his. She wouldn't look round at him. The important thing was his nearness. She would just gaze across the counter at the assistant and, like him, ask for a packet of sandwiches. She could take them home and have them for her evening meal.

She struggled up from the table but, by the time she'd retrieved her stick and started to move towards the counter, he had been served and was away. She felt so disappointed and so annoyed with herself. She ought to have known. She ought to have got up sooner. It would have been better even to stick to her original plan of going outside the moment she saw him approaching the shop and waiting and watching him. That way, at least she would have learned where either his home or his business was. She consoled herself by thinking that there would be other days and other opportunities. With a sigh, she made her way out of the shop, along to the bus stop and started the journey back home.

The house seemed more silent and oppressive than ever. She switched on the television and sat down to listen to the news. At least the television gave the illusion of company and a connection with the world outside this gloomy house and this dismal, dilapidated, graffiti-covered building.

It was the Scottish News. The announcer was saying something about a couple who'd seen what they now realised was Cheryl being kidnapped on the Balgray Hill near The Heights. Mabel's attention sharpened. She leaned forward in her chair. It had been very dark because one of the lamps had been broken. But they'd seen a man who, they thought at the time, was lifting a drunk woman into a car. Despite the darkness, they'd been able to give the police a description that it was hoped would help to find the kidnapper. He was an exceptionally tall, very thin man, they said, with hunched shoulders.

Mabel gripped the arms of her chair and fought the faintness that all but overcame her. There must be lots of men answering that description. Nevertheless, recognition accompanied by terrible, fearful thoughts jumbled about at the back of Mabel's mind. Why would a man of that description want anything to do with or have anything against Cheryl Patterson?

No matter how she fought to bury the thoughts, deny them, ridicule them even, they refused to go away. She knew. Everything became horrifyingly, terrifyingly, undeniably clear.

The announcer was giving the number of the local police and urging anyone who had any information to contact them, or *Crimewatch*. The *Crimewatch* number also came up on the screen.

Mabel leaned back against the cushions. She felt ill. She *was* ill. She was painfully breathless. Sweat was running down her face. Her heart was thumping loudly through every part of her body.

Nobody could fathom why anybody could have anything against Cheryl Patterson, of all people. Everybody in the building had said, 'Why kidnap? Why Cheryl?'

There seemed no answer. But oh, there was. A perfect answer. It was so obviously her fault. It was too terrible to think about but she couldn't stop thinking about it.

The kidnapper had mistaken Cheryl for Angela.

'God forgive me. God forgive me,' Mabel sobbed out. 'What can I do?'

The *Crimewatch* number had disappeared from the screen and she couldn't remember it. She was too afraid to phone the police in case they could trace her or question her. She would never be able to tell anyone about the shameful phone calls and how she had implicated Cheryl and put her at such risk.

It was so shameful, so wicked. Yet she must do something, anything, to help Cheryl. Gathering as much strength and calmness as she could, she tried to work out a plan. Eventually she was able to phone directory enquiries. Then, after dialling 141 so that her call could not be traced, she dialled the *Crimewatch* number.

'I know the man who kidnapped Cheryl Patterson. He lives in Bearsden. He's a Bearsden businessman. He'll have taken Cheryl to be with him in Bearsden.'

She hung up. It was the best she could do. Now all that was left was to pray that Cheryl would be found alive and well.

'Oh please God,' she kept repeating. 'Oh please God.'

33

'Changes. Changes,' Betty said.

She was down in the entrance hall saying goodbye to Rita and her children. Dorothy was giving them a lift to the new house that had been allocated to them. The children were already outside with Dorothy in the car. Rita suddenly pounced on Betty and gave her a hug. Then, suddenly embarrassed at herself, she jerked away.

'Thanks for everything.'

'I'll see you at one of our get-togethers, I hope.'

'Sure.'

Rita turned at the door and waved. Betty waved energetically back, especially to the children sitting in the car, their small faces pressed against the window.

'That another lot gone?' Monty appeared from his office, gripping a pipe at one side of his mouth.

'Uh-huh. Unfortunately there's plenty of other poor souls waiting to take their place. As long as they feel safe and able to start a new life by the time they leave here, that's the main thing. I have to get back up, Monty. Wee Mary's all excited. I'd better have a go at calming her down.'

The safe house was in chaos with cases in the lobby and jerseys and skirts and knickers and vests and tights and scarves scattered about the floor and draped over the lobby chair and door handles.

Mary said, 'Sorry about this, hen, but it's times like this when I miss my bloody arm.'

'Where's Janet?'

'In the bedroom. I flung everything out here before she could stop me. I wanted to get out of her road. She's finishing off packing her stuff. Her stuff's all that good, she's got to fold it aw in tissue paper and be awfu' careful. She likes to do things right. But she said she's going to pack my things.'

'Here, let me help you.'

'Isn't she an awfu' good soul? I couldnae have gone an' left her. She's been such a pal. But ah never thought she'd offer to come wi' me.'

'It'll be good for Janet to start a new life in another district and she's fond of you. The pair of you will get on great.'

'I know. I know. Ah can hardly believe ma luck.'

'Well, you've been waiting a long time, Mary. You were due a house.'

'Ma luck at ma pal comin' wi' me, I mean.'

'Oh well. Janet's lucky too.'

'At least she'll no' need to worry about sufferin' that husband o' hers. She told me all about him, you know. She's never spoken to anybody else but she told me. A posh company director – two-faced bastard. Ah'm that glad she's divorcing him and getting rid of him for good.'

Betty was lifting clothes and packing them into Mary's case and shopping trolley.

'You'll like the south side, Mary, and I can just see the pair of you enjoying nice walks in Queen's Park.'

'Och, ah'm that lucky, right enough.'

Just then, Janet appeared from the bedroom.

'Goodness, you've done it all.'

'Och, it wisnae me, hen. It was Betty here. She's aye been that good to me, so she has.'

'Well, that's us all ready then, just waiting for the taxi.'

Betty glanced at her watch.

'It'll be here in about ten minutes. I'll help you down with everything. Here, let me balance a couple of cases on top of Mary's trolley. Give me that big case of yours, Janet.'

Sandra had gone to her sister's in Edinburgh. Rita and the children had already left for their house. Kate and Alice now crowded around to say their goodbyes to wee Mary and Janet.

Betty had to hurry them eventually.

'Come on, you two. The taxi won't wait for ever. And I'm lumbered here.'

'Oh, I am sorry,' Janet said. 'I was forgetting you've got our heavy luggage, Betty.' She gave a quick last look at the lilac and green of the safe house before following Betty out to the landing.

The others saw them to the lift and they waved until the doors shut and the lift plummeted down. There was silence in the lift until Betty said cheerfully, 'Don't worry, folks. Their turn will come.'

★★★★★

Mabel heard the doorbell and guessed that it must be Mrs Patterson. No one else ever came to her door. She was huddled in bed and did not know how she would be able to get up. The bell didn't stop, however, and she was forced to make the effort. She dragged a cream, crocheted shawl around the shoulders of her white flannelette nightie. Then she reached for her stick.

It took her a long weary time to reach the front door.

'Oh, there you are,' Mrs Patterson said. 'I was getting worried about you. Have you sent for the doctor yet?'

She hadn't, of course. What was the use?

'Can I come in?'

Mabel opened the door wider.

'You look terrible, Miss Smith. You go back to bed and I'll make you a cup of tea.'

In a minute or two, Mrs Patterson called from the kitchen, 'Your milk's gone sour. I'll go back upstairs for some of mine. I'll leave the door open so you won't have to get up again. I won't be long.'

Mabel lay back in bed. A sense of hopelessness weighed her down. Guilt too. How could she live if Cheryl's life was taken? Cheryl had everything to live for. She was young and beautiful – as she had so often described her to John. Her eyes closed at the memory of how often, and in what detail, she'd described Cheryl to him. She couldn't bear it. Her only hope was that the police would, at this very moment, be searching Bearsden and that they would find the poor girl.

'It's me,' Mrs Patterson was calling now. 'I'm just going to make the tea.' In no time, she was through in the bedroom. carrying a tray.

'I had some rolls upstairs, so I buttered one and put a wee bit honey on it. Honey's good for you. Here, let me help you to sit up.'

She propped Mabel into a sitting position with a couple of pillows.

'There now, that's better.'

'I'm sorry. I don't think I could eat anything.'

'You must try, Miss Smith. At least drink your tea just now.'

'Has there been any news?'

'Yes, the police seem to have a good lead, thank God. They're concentrating on Bearsden. They've got sniffer dogs there and everything. I feel a bit more hopeful. Bearsden is swarming with police. My husband has been out there. Tommy too. Tommy moved in with us. He couldn't concentrate at his work or anything else, he said. He saw for himself. The police are going all out to find our Cheryl. They're doing their very best, Tommy says. We're all a bit more hopeful now.'

'I keep praying and praying,' Mabel said.

'Now, I've told you before, Miss Smith, you mustn't feel that you had anything to do with it. It wasn't anything to do with Cheryl going out for your messages. She was going out anyway. Try to drink up your tea.'

Mrs Patterson held the cup up to Mabel's lips.

'That's it. Another sip now. It'll help strengthen you. But I don't care what you say, Miss Smith. You need a doctor and I'm going to use your phone right now to call one.'

Mabel hadn't the strength to stop her. The phone call was made. The doctor was coming. The same doctor, no doubt, who had wanted to send her to an old-folks' home. Despite the guilt and helplessness, she suddenly felt alert with fear. But why should she care about what happened to her any more? But she *did* care about being shut away in some dreadful institution. She couldn't help it.

'I'll let you know immediately if there's any news,' Mrs Patterson said, 'and I'll leave your door off the latch so the doctor can just walk right in.'

Speechless with apprehension now, Mabel nodded.

*****

If it took him every day of the rest of his life, Ingram determined he'd find the evil bitch. Nothing and no one now would deny him the pleasure of killing her. The problem was to get out of his flat. The whole of Bearsden was seething with police. There were even police dogs sniffing around.

He didn't dare go near the car park to get his car. But if he could just reach the bus stop and get on a bus, he'd be safely on his way. He'd get into town, then catch another bus from there to the Balgray Hill. In one of the myriad of flats in The Heights, towering into the sky from the Balgray Hill, he'd find Angela. Even if it meant knocking on every door from the bottom flat to the top. Every single door. All he would need would be for her to open the door and say something, anything. It was by her voice that he would know her.

He kept peering out from behind the curtains of his window. He stayed hunched there from first thing in the morning until the afternoon, when a wintry darkness descended on Bearsden.

As far as he could see, the police had moved away from Drymen Road. At least from along the front of the shops. He put on his raincoat and turned up the collar. Now was the time he could take a chance and venture out. Now was the time.

Very quickly he locked his front door and crept down the stairs. Keeping his head down, he let his long legs carry him swiftly towards the bus stop.

Great! A bus was also approaching along Drymen Road. No hanging about waiting for one. He jumped on, the fare ready in his hand. As he sat on the bus, his legs twitched with impatience. Mentally he was willing the driver to stamp his foot down harder on the accelerator. He ached to scream at the man, 'Quicker, quicker, for God's sake!'

It seemed an age before he arrived at the bus station and was loping along to where he knew he would find a bus to carry him to the Balgray Hill.

At last, there was The Heights, a dark giant reaching up to the clouds. Only the occasional pinpoint of light told him of life unseen behind its windows.

Many people, Ingram realised, would still be at work. Perhaps Angela would be one of them. But he was a patient man. If necessary, he'd wait.

He couldn't wait, however, to make a start. He saw the concierge emerging from the office at the side of the entrance hall. He was biting into a large roll.

John muttered 'Evening' to the man and quickly looked away. He went over to the lift. Perhaps better to start at the top floor and work his way down. Several people emerged from the lift. Ingram kept his head lowered. Another man got into the lift before Ingram could press the button for the top floor. Ingram did not raise his eyes to see what button the man pressed.

'What floor do you want?' the man asked him.

'Top.'

'Right.' The man pressed another button.

After a couple of floors, the man got off and Ingram was left standing alone. He watched the numbers as the lift floated up higher and higher. At long last, it reached thirty and he stepped out on to a dismal-looking landing, its walls splattered with spray-painted graffiti. There were four doors.

He started pressing bells.

'I wonder if I could interest you in a new kitchen?' he asked.

'Naw,' the woman who opened the first door replied, before banging the door shut in his face.

The woman next door gave a more polite refusal. As did the third. He was about to knock at the fourth door when he noticed, just in time, the name Patterson on the name plate.

He suddenly remembered the girl had insisted her name was Cheryl Patterson and she lived on the thirtieth floor of The Heights. Sweat trickled down from his brow as he hastened over, stiff with tension and suspense, to press the button for the lift to take him quickly down to the twenty-ninth floor.

*****

Meanwhile, down below, it suddenly occurred to Monty that the Photofit description he'd seen on *Crimewatch* was a perfect march for the tall, thin man he'd seen entering the lift. His hand trembled as he reached for the phone and dialled 999.

34

Mabel didn't know how long she'd slept. She had been dozing off despite her mind being full of anxieties about the doctor's visit. She dreaded him announcing that he'd been successful in getting her 'put away'. He wouldn't use those words, of course, but that's how she thought of what he was trying to do. Banished to hell, that was another way she thought of being shut away in an institution. Maybe that's what she deserved, of course. Maybe that was going to be her punishment.

She thought she heard a noise in the lobby.

'Is that you, Doctor?' she called out.

After a moment's silence a voice suddenly roared out, 'Angela!'

John's voice.

Horror grabbed her by the throat. She couldn't utter a sound.

She heard the door crash back. Then a scuffle of feet and John cursing and shouting, 'I want to see her. I need to see her.'

Another man's voice said, 'You're not seeing anybody. You're coming with us.'

Footsteps retreating, then complete silence.

*****

Not long afterwards the doctor appeared at the bedroom door.

'I got your neighbour's phone message. Now let's see how you are.'

'Oh, Doctor. . .' She was still finding it difficult to speak. Already he was taking her madly racing pulse. Then, after he had sounded her chest and found her heart thumping erratically, he peeled the stethoscope from his neck. He looked at her seriously.

'You've had more than enough shocks and worry. The quicker we get you away from here the better. I've managed to get you considered for one of the council places. I'll write the address down for you. I've given them all your particulars and they're sending someone to see you later. You're going to be all right. Meantime I'll give you something to calm you down.'

He was away before she could recover from her trauma. He had always been such a brusque man and never had much time to chat with his patients. Nor listen to them, it seemed. He was an extremely busy man, of course.

A few minutes later, Mrs Patterson arrived.

'I'll go and get your prescription,' she told Mabel. 'The quicker you start it, the better. The doctor was saying on the phone he was getting you into some place where you'd be safer. I'm pleased about that, aren't you? I mean, you could fall or anything could happen while you're on your own here.'

Mabel didn't know what to say. Life was getting all too much for her. She was still in shock after hearing John's voice and then him being arrested.

When Mrs Patterson left, Mabel forced herself to get up and put on some clothes. A woman had phoned from the council place and she wanted to look independent when the woman arrived. That way the council might be persuaded that she didn't need 'put away' after all.

When the doorbell rang, she made her way as best she could along the lobby to open the door to the woman. But it was a man standing at the door. She knew she'd seen him before but, for a few seconds, she couldn't quite place him.

'It's Tommy, Miss Smith. Cheryl's boyfriend.'

'Oh yes. Come in, Tommy. Has there been any news of Cheryl?'

Tommy followed her slow progress back along the lobby and into the sitting room.

'Well, yes. I'm hoping something will come of this.'

He sat down in the chair opposite Mabel.

'You know Monty, the concierge?'

'Yes.'

'Well, he saw this strange guy come into the foyer and he realised he answered the description that had been given out. You know – a very tall thin man with shoulders hunched forward. So he phoned the police. They came immediately and took him away for questioning. I'm praying that he's the one and they'll find out from him where Cheryl is.'

'Oh, thank goodness,' Mabel said. 'Oh, thank you so much for telling me, Tommy. That was very thoughtful of you. I'm so relieved. I feel sure you'll soon have her back now.'

His young face lit up. 'Do you think so? It'll be so wonderful if I get her back safe and well. Talk about relief! I've been nearly demented. I'll never let her out of my sight again.'

'Yes, I'm sure.'

She smiled at him and he rose.

'Do you mind if I push off again, Miss Smith? I want to go and try to find out if there've been any more developments. The police said they'd let us know but I can't bear to wait.'

'Yes, on you go, son. And thank you again.'

With a wave he was gone. The outside door banged shut. She was left feeling relieved and glad, yet at the same time not sure at all. She was relieved the police had got John and she felt sure they'd find out from him where he'd taken Cheryl. They would find Cheryl but would she be alive and well?

'Oh please God. Oh please God.'

*****

Cheryl could hear the occasional gurgle of water. The icy dampness that had been seeping into the very marrow of her bones now added to her terror. Was she near a stream or a river? Could it be that somewhere near, water was slowly rising, ready to engulf her?

Already she was as cold as death. In a frantic effort to keep alive, she tried to kick her tightly bound feet backwards and forwards. Desperately she struggled to twist her body from side to side. But weakness and exhaustion from lack of food and water soon dragged her back down into hopelessness. The foul fusty smell of the place made her retch uselessly to one side. In the heavy silent blackness of the place she felt death creeping closer.

'Tommy.' Her mind formed the word before sliding into unconsciousness.

*****

When the woman from the council place arrived, Mabel's mind was still so fixed on Cheryl and the suspense of waiting to hear any more news about her that she couldn't concentrate or really care much what the woman was saying. She tried to be at least polite, however, and even offered to make a cup of tea.

'No, no,' the woman said, 'don't worry, dear. I think I've got all the information I need now. Fortunately there's a very nice place vacant at the moment. You'll be getting a letter very soon. No, just sit where you are. I'll see myself out.'

The woman was right. The letter came the very next day giving an 'appointment to view'. Transport would be provided, it said. Mabel tried not to feel as if she was on her way to hell. After all, she told herself, just because she went to 'view' surely didn't mean she'd be forced to stay.

Later, she'd just been coming out of the lift on her way towards the 'transport', when Tommy burst into the foyer and yelled out, 'They've found her! They've found her! She's in hospital but she's going to be all right. I'm rushing to tell her mum and dad and take them with me to see her.'

He raced across the foyer and disappeared into the lift before Mabel could express the intensity of her relief. Tears blurred her eyes as she made her way outside. She didn't care now if she *was* on her way to hell or *what* happened to her. Cheryl was safe. That was all that mattered.

The private car that the council had sent sped her away to the opposite end of the city. She relaxed back, allowing the relief to keep washing over her.

'Here we are,' the driver was saying. 'Out you come.' He helped her from the car. She looked around and found herself on the drive of a large block of very modern-looking flats.

'Nice, aren't they?' The driver cupped her elbow with his hand. 'The manager will show you around.'

At the main door of the building, he pressed the bell and spoke into a security panel.

'It's Bert with Miss Smith.'

In a few minutes, the door opened and a pleasant-looking woman was smiling at her.

'I'll leave you to it then,' Bert said and off he went, whistling cheerfully.

'I'm Mrs Anderson, the manager. Molly, if you'd rather.' She laughed. 'Molly the Manager, most of them call me. Come on up and welcome. I'll show you first of all up to the flat.'

'Flat?' Mabel echoed in confusion.

'Here's the lift ready and waiting.'

A group of elderly men and women were emerging from the lift, chatting and laughing. One of them said, 'Hello, Molly.'

'Come on, you lot, out of my way.'

The others laughed again and one of them said, 'Cheeky old devil.'

'Here you, less of the old. I'm a young thing compared to you lot.'

The lift doors shut and Molly said, 'There's three floors but the flat that's empty just now is one up.'

Out of the lift, Molly led Mabel across to a door that she opened with a key.

Mabel looked around inside with mounting disbelief. It was a lovely bright flat with a bathroom, a kitchen, a sitting room and one bedroom. In the little square hall and in each room, as well as the kitchen and bathroom, there was a red cord hanging loose.

Molly explained, 'If you have any trouble or worry about anything, or if you fall, you just pull one of the cords and I'll come immediately, or if I'm off duty – although I do live in the place – a carer will come to help. Everybody gets a pendant to wear as well, so that if anybody doesn't happen to be near a cord, all that's needed is to press the button on the pendant. Then of course I phone each flat every morning to check that everybody's OK.'

'Goodness!' Mabel said.

'Do you like the flat, then?'

'Oh, it's lovely.'

'OK then, you can move in as soon as you like. Come on down to the common room and meet some of the others. But don't get me wrong. You never need to have anything to do with anybody else, if you don't want to. But there's a tea bar there and I usually join everyone for elevenses. You know, a wee cup of tea or coffee and a blether. And of course we have different things always going on if you're interested – sewing bees, bingo nights, whatever we can think up to keep everybody cheery. Here we are. It's just along the corridor. Take your time now. There's no hurry.'

Everybody was sitting in a circle on comfortable cushioned chairs in pretty shades of blue and red. They were happily chatting and drinking from floral mugs.

'Here we are,' Molly called out. 'Another new pal for you. Mabel Smith.'

'Hello, Mabel' and 'Welcome' were called out.

'There, now!' Molly helped her gently into a seat. 'What'll you have then? I'm the best tea and coffee maker in the business.'

Mabel gazed up at Molly's plump, kindly face. It was then she realised without a doubt that, far from being in hell, she was in heaven.

THE END